Also by Micheal Maxwell

Cole Sage Mysteries
Diamonds and Cole
Cellar of Cole
Helix of Cole
Cole Dust
Cole Shoot
Cole Fire
Heart of Cole
Cole Mine
Soul of Cole
Cole Cuts

Adam Dupree Mysteries
Dupree's Rebirth
Dupree's Reward
Dupree's Resolve

Flynt and Steele Mysteries
(Written with Warren Keith)
Dead Beat
Dead Duck
Dead on Arrival

Copyright © 2020 by Micheal Maxwell

All rights reserved. No part of this book may be reproduced in any form or by any means, electronic or mechanical, including photocopying, recording, or by any information storage and retrieval system, without permission in writing from the publisher.

ISBN: 9798666254219

CELLAR OF COLE

MICHEAL MAXWELL

ONE

Phillip Wesley Ashcroft was a man of peculiar habits, a bachelor, not by personal choice, but by the choice of what seemed to be the entire female sex. He lived alone. He had few, if any, friends, and a family that would just as soon pretend he didn't exist. At work, he did what was expected and not much more. He arrived at exactly 8:55 A.M. and left promptly at 5:05 P.M.

He carried a red plaid lunch bag that zipped open to reveal a matching plaid thermos with a bright screw-off cap that doubled as a cup. In the thermos were the boiling hot contents of a can of Campbell's Chicken Noodle soup heated each morning on the back left-hand burner of his stove. He never added the can of water as the directions instructed; he preferred his soup full strength. The bit of broth that wouldn't fit in the thermos was added to a container kept in the freezer compartment of his refrigerator, to be used at some future date.

In a clear Ziploc sandwich bag, he packed seven saltine crackers—no more, no less. He would lay the bag on the lunchroom table and smash the crackers with the butt of his hand. After adding the bits to the soup, he would turn the bag inside out and lick the bottom seam. He delighted in the salty powder that was left behind. This daily ritual was unobserved by his fellow employees because Phillip Wesley Ashcroft always took lunch alone.

Although he found his work tedious, he seldom missed a day and, in fact, hadn't bothered to take a vacation for the last three years in a row. Phillip Wesley Ashcroft occupied the same grey-carpeted cubicle for the past sixteen years. Once or twice a year, he brought a handheld vacuum cleaner to the office and thoroughly vacuumed all the carpeted surfaces.

Few things annoyed Phillip Wesley Ashcroft. By and large, he was lacking in malice. However, he hated the hairs on his fingers. He shaved them, waxed them, and even tried burning them off with a soldering iron, one hair at a time, but they always grew back. He hated the way he could see them when he bit his nails.

He also hated his thick body hair. This was probably the result of the resentment he felt for going bald at a young age. He bought infomercial goo to remove it. Twenty years ago, for almost a year, he had a smooth body. Arms, legs, back, even parts that chafed and burned from the shaving and chemicals. He shaved his head, his eyebrows, and even plucked out his eyelashes. It took almost an entire day to get clean and smooth. But he did it. It was no use, though. It all grew back. The worst part was the itching. When it got to be about an eighth of an inch long, it almost drove him insane. So, he gave up. But his hands and fingers were different. Those *had* to be smooth.

CELLAR OF COLE

Each night he washed them three times. He cleaned under his nails, or what was left of them, and applied lotion. He wore soft cotton gloves to bed and, in the morning, gently moisturized his hands with a lanolin-glycerin mixture he developed over several years. For a while, he thought of bottling and selling his mixture and even designed a label, but he gave up the idea.

Today, the hair on his hands was particularly annoying him. *I must think of something else.* Phillip Wesley Ashcroft loved to play "thought games." He delighted in knowing that he was miles away, deep inside his own world of words, and that if anyone were to walk by his cubicle, it would look like he was hard at work. Not like some of the people around him who played solitaire or Tetris on their computers. They always got caught, scolded, and told not to do it anymore—but they always did. Not Phillip Wesley Ashcroft, though. He was never scolded because there was no way to catch him. Except on rare occasions when his supervisor came to review his current project, no one bothered him. No one knew he was playing his own special games in his head.

Today's game would be based on something he thought about on the bus to work. Today he would play with names. Not just any names, but names of people like himself who were referred to by all three of their names. Lee Harvey Oswald killed Kennedy. That was too easy, too obvious, he must try harder. John Wayne Gacy killed boys, painted clowns. Phillip Wesley Ashcroft thought Gacy was a pervert. *Who killed the other Kennedy?* he thought. Sirhan Sirhan, only two names. He smiled as he wondered if Sirhan's middle name was also Sirhan.

James Earl Ray shot Martin Luther King and claimed he was innocent to the end. *Who else?* Phillip Wesley Ashcroft thought as he shuffled the papers in front of him. John Wilkes Booth killed Lincoln. Billy Bob Thornton, who was he? Who did he kill? *Stupid*, Phillip Wesley Ashcroft thought to himself, *he's an actor; he didn't kill anybody.* Neither, for that matter, did Billy Ray Cyrus.

The guy who killed John Lennon was known by all three of his names, but Phillip Wesley Ashcroft took a vow to never speak them. Many famous murderers committed their crime to become famous, like the guy who killed Lennon. Phillip Wesley Ashcroft would steal his fame, or at least a small part of it, by never speaking his name. He tried not to even think it. That way, he would remember the Beatle, but his killer would fade away because he would be nameless.

Henry Lee Lucas confessed to 3,000 killings, but the number was closer to 200. Tommy Lynn Sells said he killed 70. His favorite, though, was Jack "The" Ripper. Phillip Wesley Ashcroft giggled softly to himself for his cleverness. *"The,"* he thought, *was the perfect middle name.* He ended the game on a happy note.

Phillip Wesley Ashcroft started using all three of his names in 1991 when he read in the newspaper of Donald Henry "Pee Wee" Gaskins. Phillip Wesley Ashcroft loved the way the paper referred to him as "the meanest man in America." Gaskins confessed to more than 200 murders but was convicted of only nine. Phillip Wesley Ashcroft bought Gaskins' autobiography online and read with complete clarity and understanding of Gaskins' claim that he possessed "a special mind" that gave him "permission to kill."

That "special mind" was something Phillip Wesley Ashcroft shared with Pee Wee Gaskins. Although he never committed a murder, the time was drawing near. It would be a release to finally fulfill what he was put on Earth to do. The evil that crept over society was corrupting and perverting all things sweet and pure. Phillip Wesley Ashcroft spent hours worrying and watching as children passed in front of his apartment on their way to school each morning. He feared they would be corrupted somehow before they could make it to the safety of the classroom.

School was a safe place for Phillip Wesley Ashcroft. Mrs. Smith, Mrs. Duncan, and Miss Cotton all treated him like he was special. *Children need protection from parents who spank them for no reason,* he thought. At school, there were no cold baths to teach you not to wet the bed. There were no endless rantings about the value of a dime-sized splash of milk on the table. At school, you didn't have to eat raw rice so you would value the hard work mommy took to cook your meals. At school, there was milk and graham crackers and a pat on the head for a job well done. Phillip Wesley Ashcroft loved school.

Children were much nicer than adults. He missed the nice little girls who would pass him notes in class. He missed the cookie or piece of candy they would give him from their lunch pails. How did those nice little girls grow up to be the short-tempered bitches that now surrounded him? Just let him make a mistake on a report or be late with an audit review, and watch their fangs come out.

The boys always invited him to play catch or dodge ball at recess. They would all ride their bikes home after school and pretend they were flying in formation like the Blue Angels. They never invited him for a drink after work now, did they? No jokes for him to hear at the soda machines, no lunchtime dash to the taqueria with a buddy, so he ate alone, ignored.

The answer was in the children. If they were preserved while they were still sweet and pure, they could be saved. They simply could not be allowed to grow into cold, distant, unfeeling adults. Phillip Wesley Ashcroft had no need for the fairy tale world of heaven. He knew there was nothing out there. No pearly gates, no sweet by and by, and certainly no streets paved in gold. There was just rest, perfect rest. The darkness and peace you feel in a deep motionless sleep; that is what awaits you when your heartbeat stops. That is what he could offer the children—the peace and the assurance of remaining innocent.

Phillip Wesley Ashcroft turned and looked at Beth Swann in the cubicle across the aisle. She was so involved in her own world of work, parties, and friends that she had no time for him. Not that she was his ideal. She was too thin, her hair was too straight, and she had a bump on the bridge of her nose. That didn't stop a constant stream of men from passing by just to say "hi" to Beth and look down the front of her blouse. They would share a story about a coworker, a pleasantry about a recent party or reception and, more often than not, inquire as to her social calendar for the weekend. It made him sick.

When she first came to the office, Phillip Wesley Ashcroft asked her to dinner. "So sorry" was her response; there was "a previous engagement." That didn't stop her from accepting an invitation from Martin Mauer five minutes later. Three years passed and she never looked in his direction, never offered him a cookie or piece of candy from her lunch pail. She grew up. She would have been much nicer twenty or so years earlier. He just knew it.

TWO

The Chicago wind roared around corners like a freight train down a mountain. The sidewalks were icy and slick and the air seared the inside of your nostrils like razor burn, but to Cole Sage, it could have been a day in May. Like a blind man getting back his sight or a lame man who once again could walk, Cole was a man reborn.

It was a little over six months since Ellie died. She was in his heart and on his mind for most of his adult life. They parted long ago and were reunited only for a few days, but in those few days, he found a new life. The love and longing he felt for her, she felt just as deeply half a continent away. Even though the longing to be together was never to be realized, they did have one great connection: a daughter. Erin was a smart, beautiful young woman that Cole hadn't known existed.

The joy of having a part of Ellie live on was like an emotional heart transplant. In the few days before her passing, they were able to share soul-deep emotion and unfiltered feelings that few people ever experience. Ellie freed Cole of the pain and remorse of losing her all those years ago and showed him that his life could mean something. Erin had become such a wonderful part of his life that sometimes he couldn't remember the years he spent alone.

His work went from drudgery to a laser light of committed dedication. The series he wrote on the alarming number of elderly people turning to violence was being considered for a Pulitzer Prize, then was picked up and reprinted in dozens of magazines and newspapers throughout the United States and Canada. Offers of book deals, radio and television interviews, and jobs—to the point where Cole hired a manager. But he wasn't just on a crusade for the elderly. It was just the rekindling of the journalistic fire he almost destroyed with apathy and cynicism.

Cole's co-workers at the *Sentinel* weren't quite sure what to make of this "new" member of their staff. He greeted people with a friendly smile, the scowl, that served as such a valuable mask, was gone, and his trademark rapier wit returned quicker, funnier, and more topical than ever. He became the textbook example of the multi-tasker. Many of the younger writers on the paper never knew the young Cole. Their mental picture of that nasty guy in the end cubicle was their only experience.

This new Cole looked different, too. He had lost weight, about 25 pounds, so that instead of looking 10 years older than his 45 years, he now looked 10 years younger, a change that did not go unnoticed by female members of the staff, which led to the speculation around the third floor newsroom that Cole had found a new lady. You could say that was the case. He actually delighted in *two* new ladies in his life: his daughter, Erin, and his granddaughter, Jenny. But for now, that was just for a few close friends to know.

Cole shook off the snow and stamped his feet as he entered the outside lobby of the *Sentinel* building. The trappings of Thanksgiving oranges and browns gave way to the greens and reds of the Christmas season. A bright red banner with sparkling gold lettering offering "Season's Greetings" in several languages was draped on the wall above the reception area. Cole crossed the lobby on the slip-proof rubber mats that were installed across the marble floor to prevent falls and the lawsuits that followed.

"It's beginning to look a lot like Christmas," Cole sang as he approached the pretty blonde receptionist.

"Season's greetings!" she offered in her bubbly best.

"Merry Christmas!" Cole returned.

The blonde scowled at Cole as if he had just blurted out some unpleasant profanity. She was programmed to be politically correct and took her charge very seriously.

"How do you know I'm not Jewish, Mr. Sage?"

"Well, then, Happy Hanukkah!" Cole offered cheerfully as he passed her.

"That's not my point," she said, still scowling.

Cole stopped and turned to the angry receptionist. "We cannot impose our value system on others, it can cause real emotional harm," she lectured.

"First, what is your name? I don't think I know it." Cole was still smiling.

"Breanna."

"Okay, Breanna, I hope you have a strong sense of self-worth and a positive self-image because I intend to do you 'real emotional harm.'" Cole cleared his throat and began singing in a loud clear voice:

"Silent night, holy night
Shepherds quake at the sight
Glories stream from heaven afar
Heavenly hosts sing alleluia
Christ the Savior is born
Christ the Savior is born."

Cole smiled, cleared his throat again and stood as if awaiting approval.

"Is that supposed to be funny?"

"Nope, it was supposed to be "Silent Night." You see, this is December 6, and in 19 days it will be Christmas Day, the 25th of December, the day that is recognized the whole world 'round as the day Jesus Christ was born—even though he probably was born sometime in the spring. In case you haven't heard, He's the guy who started a religion that—the last time I checked—is practiced by the majority of the people of the United States of America, the country in which we are currently residing. Now, in the off chance that you are truly, and not jokingly, a member of the proud and historical Jewish faith—because joking about that would be truly offensive and could cause real emotional harm—this is for you:

Oh Hanukkah, Oh Hanukkah, come light the Menorah,
Let's have a party; we'll all dance the hora.
Gather 'round the table, we'll give you a treat.
S'vivon to play with, Latkes to eat."

The receptionist was stone-faced. "I don't think you're funny, Mr. Sage."

"That's good because I was trying to make a point. People like you make me puke with your self-righteous inflexible desire to make the rest of us conform to your vision of equality. Obviously, you are neither a believer in Christ, since you failed to sing along with "Silent Night" and whose birthday you would be happily celebrating, but more importantly, you wouldn't have started this silly conversation in the first place. Nor are you proud to be of the Jewish faith since you didn't wish me a Happy Hanukkah when I offered—or smart enough to be a Buddhist and just keep your mouth shut because you would realize my faith is my way to enlightenment and no business of yours. So, I figure you're just a stupid sheep following what some professor somewhere told you."

The blonde just sat with eyes bugged out, slack-jawed at Cole's reaction.

"Oh, yeah, and one more thing, Breanna. If you really want to be politically correct, you will let your hair go back to its natural dark brown color, because as a fellow member of the brunette community, your disenfranchisement and rejection of your natural color to me is very hurtful and emotionally harmful. But you won't do that, will you?"

"I think—"

"Frankly, I don't want to hear it. Merry Christmas!" Cole brightly said. Then he smiled, swiped his ID card, and went through the employee's entrance behind the reception desk.

"Kwanzaa yenu iwe na heri, Olajean!" Cole said, trying to give his old friend a high five.

"What is with you? You know I'm Baptist!"

"I was just trying to be sensitive to your African roots and let you know that I celebrate your freedom from the slave mentality." Cole smiled slyly.

"African roots, my big black butt. Any fool knows most of the slaves brought here were from West Africa. This Kwanzaa stuff is all about East African rituals. First fruits and all. It ain't got no Christian foundation. Ain't about my Jesus' birthday. I ain't havin' it, no sir! I'm talkin' 'bout the birth of my Lord, that's all!"

"I just love to hear you preach, Olajean."

"You're just tryin' to rile me up, Cole Sage. You should be ashamed. You know how I get. You go on and get to your office." Olajean folded her arms across her massive chest and stuck out her bottom lip in an effort to look hurt.

Cole leaned way over the counter and kissed her on the top of her head. "That's why I love you. You know exactly what you believe and aren't afraid to shout it."

"Little church wouldn't do you no harm. A little shoutin', neither. Christmas service is 7 o'clock! I'll save you a seat!"

"Sorry, got plans."

"What? Watchin' Scrooge on TV?"

"No, I'm going to see my daughter and her family out in California."

"Oh, Cole, that is so wonderful. I was hoping you might."

"Yep, I'll be there on the 22nd. If you're nice to me, I might bring you back a bag of big, sweet California oranges."

"I'm brown sugar from now on," Olajean said, reaching for the flashing red phone line on her console. She blew Cole a kiss and gave him a dismissive wave.

When Cole got to his cubicle, he noticed the stack of pink message slips stuck all over his keyboard. He took off his overcoat, scarf, leather jacket, and Russian fox fur hat, and sat down.

"So, what have we got here?" Cole started sorting through the stack. Three return calls from potential interviewees, one from a Wichita television station, a call from the payroll office about insurance deductions, and one that caught Cole's attention: Chuck Waddell called from San Francisco. Chuck and Cole went all the way back to college journalism classes. The last he heard, Chuck was working as the London Office Chief for the Dallas Morning News. Cole reached for the phone and punched in the number, eager to catch up with his old friend.

"*Chronicle.* What extension?"

"Chuck Waddell, please."

"Mr. Waddell is on another line; care to hold?"

"Sure."

Cole was able to hear a medley from *Cats* and a smooth jazz version of "Little Drummer Boy" before Chuck came on the line.

"Cole, how are you? How're things in Popsicle Land?"

"Warm and toasty where I'm sitting, but your California cotton wardrobe wouldn't do you much good back here. Temperature on the bank sign says, 'Too cold, going in to warm up.' It's about 20 degrees, but with the wind chill, it's about 5 below. Want to come back for some water polo?"

"No, thanks. What's this I hear about Brennan being sick?"

"Not good. Started last summer with a chest cold, he thought. Couldn't shake it. Turns out its cancer. He's a fighter, you know, but the chemo has knocked him for a loop. Still coming to work every day, but I don't know how long he can keep up."

"I'm sorry. I know he means a lot to you."

"Thanks, Chuck. How's Chris?"

"He's fine. Into some kind of Burmese cooking this month. Got my guts churning. Too many veggies for me, I'm a steak-and-potatoes guy, ya know? Otherwise, we're fine. I'll send you a picture of our remodel with your Christmas card."

"Cool."

There was a long awkward silence. Usually, Cole and Chuck could keep the phone lines buzzing for ages before the pause set in.

Cole spoke first. "So, why do I get the feeling there is more to this call than a friendly hello. When did you get back from London, and what are you doing at the *Chronicle*?"

"Got back in July. Dallas wasn't a good fit anymore. San Francisco is wonderful, and I love my new job. That's why I'm calling, really."

"Oh, yeah?"

"Aren't you about due for a change of climate? How long has it been? Thirteen or fourteen years?"

"Twelve this time," Cole said thoughtfully.

"I'll cut to the chase. I got a spot out here. I want you for it, and I've got the budget. What's it gonna take?" Waddell was matter-of-fact, but Cole could envision his broad smile at the other end of the line.

"Well, 'Happy Holidays' to you, too."

"I'm serious, Cole. We've got a great staff, and the editorial team is actually a team. No infighting around here. I need someone to write 'heart' stuff. Your stuff. Dig up the crap and show the human side, the effects, and damage. You're what we need here. Sort of the capper."

"What are you, the editor?"

"No. Associate. But everybody knows we're friends and well, I sort of . . . ."

"You said you could get me."

"Something like that."

"I bet."

"Look, I'll send you a first-class ticket and put you up at the St. Francis if you just come out, meet the team, and give us a legitimate chance to win you over."

"Burmese dinner?"

"Whatever you want," Waddell said excitedly.

Since Ellie's death, Cole had reevaluated his life. Mick Brennan gave him a job after he got fired from the *Journal*. Nobody else wanted him. His work stunk. Cole knew it, and anybody with an eighth-grade education knew it. The fire went out. Brennan gave him a job and, as much as he hated Chicago, a home. His torment over losing Ellie all those years ago—call it foolish, call it an excuse—sent him into a professional limbo for a dozen years. Now the curse was lifted. She forgave him. He forgave himself. Cole Sage had set himself on fire with enthusiasm, and when the crowd gathered to watch, he gave them something to read that was electric. Maybe San Francisco would make the comeback complete. To be honest, though, the itch to give it a try was Erin and her family nearby in California.

"All right. It's a deal!"

"When can you come?"

"How about the 20th? I have plans on the 22nd in Southern California. Are two days enough?"

"That would be great!" Waddell sounded like he wasn't expecting a 'yes' and was overjoyed with Cole's willingness to consider an offer.

"Big money, huh?"

"I didn't say that!" Waddell chuckled.

"Then it better be an awfully good dinner."

"I'll tell Chris to keep practicing. Hope I can survive it."

"It'll be good to see you."

"Hey, this is business, not personal." Chuck was trying to do his best Vito Corleone.

"Hey, Chuck," Cole interrupted.

"Yeah?"

"Thanks for thinking of me."

"Look for the FedEx boy in the cute shorts to bring you a holiday package."

"I'll only recognize him if he takes his coat off. See you in a couple weeks."

Cole hung up, turned his chair, and looked at the picture of Erin, Jenny, and Ben that was push-pinned to the grey carpeting of the cubicle wall.

"Wouldn't that be something?" Cole said to the picture.

THREE

On Saturday, Phillip Wesley Ashcroft bought a dog, a tiny ball of curls with big eyes and a wet nose. Although he hated pink, he also bought a pink leash with a pink rhinestone collar. *It is an all-together sissy-looking thing*, he thought, *but it will suit my purposes nicely.* What child could resist a puppy? And what could be less threatening than a puppy with a pink-and-rhinestone collar and leash?

Phillip Wesley Ashcroft hated the dog. It whined and yelped all night, made messes on the floor, spilled the milk he put out in a small bowl and knocked most of the little brown balls of dog food from the bigger bowl. The animal brought bad odors and disarray to his very controlled home environment. He would get rid of it very soon. First, the creature had a job to do.

Sunday afternoon was bright and crisp. The storm that passed through on Friday and Saturday left the air clean and the sky a deep, cloudless blue. Phillip Wesley Ashcroft dressed in an uncustomary pair of brown corduroy jeans, a Cal Berkeley Bears sweatshirt, and a pair of tennis shoes. He ran the pants and sweatshirt, as well as a new Green Peace baseball cap, through the wash. He washed and dried his new clothes on high heat to take the "new" look out of them. As he dressed, he felt very uncomfortable not wearing his usual attire of sharply creased slacks and crisply laundered button-down shirt.

After a lunch of corn chips and a tuna sandwich, Phillip Wesley Ashcroft clipped the pink leash onto the rhinestone collar and left for the park with his new puppy. It took several weeks to find the perfect neighborhood park. Not far from St. Mary's School was a park with lots of kids and very few parents. It was the kind of place where parents in the neighborhood felt safe letting their children go in the company of a friend or older sibling. Most of the kids gathered around the brightly colored giraffe, the elephant climbing bars, or the bright blue spiral snake slide. A few were running and chasing each other around the lawn, but most played in the big oval sandy play area.

Near the edge of the park was a wooden bench that backed onto a thickly wooded lot. Phillip Wesley Ashcroft slipped unnoticed into the trees on Wednesday evening after work. He took a small penlight and found that the other side of the lot opened into a short side street with one house that was boarded up and another, unoccupied, that was being renovated. He walked the length of the street up one side and back down the other without seeing signs of life in any of the houses.

At the edge of the park, Phillip Wesley Ashcroft set down the dog and slipped a plastic sandwich bag over his hand to give the appearance of a dog owner conscientious enough to pick up after his pet. He casually strolled along the sidewalk in front of the park, talking to the dog in phrases and tones that truly repulsed him, but that he was sure would be in character for a man who owned the little perky ball of happiness that pranced at the end of the pink leash.

As he made his way along the park, no one paid him any attention. One man, who was probably in the park with his kids, dozed on a blanket about 30 feet from the sandy play area. A young mother, nursing an infant, sat cross-legged next to a stroller on the opposite side from the sleeping man.

Phillip Wesley Ashcroft made his way around the park and took a seat on the bench; neither adult looked up. With a quick motion, he unclipped the leash from the dog's collar. The puppy bounced and chirped around his feet. He slowly and carefully pushed the dog. As it darted back and forth, it worked its way farther and farther from where Phillip Wesley Ashcroft sat. Before too long, the sound of the children laughing and screaming in the play area caught the dog's attention. Just as he hoped, the dog ran straight for the children.

Back and forth, happily barking and spinning, the dog tried to jump up onto the concrete curb that held back the sand. Twice it rolled head over heels in the excitement of trying to reach the children. Then, just as he had imagined over and over sitting in his cubicle at work, a little girl noticed the dog.

She sat alone at the top of a deep blue spiral slide, rocking back and forth, her arms locked around the safety bars. She stretched her neck trying to get a better look at the little, curly puppy. A big smile spread across her face, exposing a big space that would soon be home to a new front tooth. At first, she stood and shifted back and forth, watching the dog. Then with one swift movement, she shot down the slide and into the sand below.

The little girl ran straight to where the puppy struggled to get into the sandbox. She stood still at the edge of the cement barrier and looked about for someone who could belong to the dog. She didn't even look in Phillip Wesley Ashcroft's direction. Satisfied, she squatted down and said something unheard to the puppy. Tentatively, she reached out and stroked the top of the dog's head, her hand jerking back when it rose up to lick her. Again she reached out and this time stroked the dog's back. The animal calmed and lay down in the grass.

Growing bolder with the dog's less frantic movements, she reached out and picked up the puppy. Gently, she rocked it back and forth in her arms, and even from his vantage point, Phillip Wesley Ashcroft could tell she was singing to the puppy. *Such sweetness,* he thought, *certainly not the actions of the woman she will become.* She would be just the kind of child he could save.

The little girl walked the perimeter of the play area, her back to Phillip Wesley Ashcroft. As she rounded the halfway mark, he stood and made his way toward her. They met just as she completed the circle.

"There you are," he said in a concerned voice.

"Is she yours?" the little girl asked.

"Yes, I was sitting on the bench over there and she ran away. I was getting ready to give her a treat and she just scampered off. Looks like she's made a new friend." Phillip Wesley Ashcroft smiled warmly.

"She's the cutest puppy I've ever seen. What's her name?"

Phillip Wesley Ashcroft stood still as a stone. He had role played this scene hundreds of times as he lay in bed drifting to sleep, but he never thought of giving the dog a name. He felt no affection for the animal and never spoke to it except in exasperation. His mind raced. Fido, Rover, Fluffy, Scruffy, Patches—they all sounded so contrived. He coughed and cleared his throat.

"You know, I haven't named her yet. Would you like to help me?" He didn't breathe until she jumped up and down and squealed.

"Please, please, please! Yes, can I name her?" the girl pleaded in delight.

Phillip Wesley Ashcroft felt the trap close. He had her. She would do anything for him now. This was better than he could have imagined.

"Let's go sit down. I still haven't given her the treats I bought. Would you like to give her some?" He bent down to look her in the face and smiled.

"Can I really feed her?"

"Sure." Phillip Wesley Ashcroft began moving toward the bench.

The girl half walked, half skipped in front of him. Phillip Wesley Ashcroft looked over at the man still napping on the blanket, he didn't move. The nursing mother switched breasts and was giving all of her attention to re-snapping and straightening her blouse.

He watched as the little girl made her way to the bench. She wore a pair of suede boots trimmed in fake lamb's wool, the legs of her jeans tucked into the tops of the boots. Her pale pink jacket had a hood with a white fluffy trim. The hood bounced in time as she skipped along.

At the bench, she spun around and hopped up onto the seat. Her pale blue-grey eyes danced as Phillip Wesley Ashcroft approached the bench and sat next to her.

"My name is Brad," he lied. He was surprised he said it. 'Brad' was his "special name," the name he used when, on those rare occasions, he tried to pick up women.

"I'm Angela. Nice to meet you." *She obviously comes from well-mannered parents*, he thought.

He reached for the small brown paper bag at the end of the bench. He was still wearing the plastic sandwich bag on his hand. He pulled out a small, unopened package of *Puppy Pretzels*. Angela chattered excitedly next to him, but he couldn't seem to focus on what she was saying. He tore the top of the package and shook several of the twisted treats into his palm. He looked at the shapes for a moment and thought they were too fat to be real pretzels.

"Here you are." He offered the treats in his right hand while gently slipping his left arm behind her along the top of the bench.

"How about Taffy?" Angela said, looking up at him with a big toothless grin.

"I don't think candy is good for puppies," he said in mock seriousness.

"I mean for a name, silly!" Angela giggled.

"Oh," Phillip Wesley Ashcroft chuckled, "I think that's a fine name. I love taffy."

Angela wiggled on the seat and worked her hand into her jacket pocket. A moment later, she extended her hand toward Phillip Wesley Ashcroft. In her palm was a piece of salt-water taffy wrapped in the traditional waxy translucent paper.

"For me?" Phillip Wesley Ashcroft felt a lump come up in his throat. A piece of candy! Just as he remembered from childhood. A pretty little girl sitting on a bench was offering him a piece of candy. She was the right choice. He nearly wept.

"I pick out just the peanut butter ones, 'cause I don't like peppermint."

"They're my favorites, too." He took the candy from her small hand. "Can I save it for later? I haven't had lunch yet."

Angela giggled.

"What?"

"You sound like my mom," Angela replied and, in a nasal singsong voice said, "Don't eat candy before dinner!" She laughed again. "Here, Taffy, have a treat." She gave the puppy one pretzel.

"How old are you, Angela?"

"Seven." Her missing tooth gave her a pronounced lisp.

"The perfect age," Phillip Wesley Ashcroft said more to himself than to the little girl beside him. "We must be neighbors, I live right over there." He pointed in the general direction of the house across the street.

"I live in San Carlos. I'm staying with my cousins for the weekend while my mommy and daddy are in Tahoe."

"Are they playing in the park, too?"

"Over there. They're boys, so they play too rough for me." She pointed and laughed as the puppy tried to lick her face. "I mostly play by myself."

Phillip Wesley Ashcroft watched as Angela teased the dog playfully with a pretzel then gently let the dog take it from her fingertips. He poured three more pieces into her hand. Her hair seemed to sparkle as the sun hit the nearly white shine of her golden blonde tips. He felt the warmth of winter sun on his face and for a moment closed his eyes, enjoying the nearness of another human being.

"I think she's full," Angela said.

The puppy lay quietly in her lap with its eyes closed; it was also enjoying the sun and the softness of Angela's presence. She gently stroked the little curly mass as its breath grew heavier.

"I think Taffy is falling asleep," Angela whispered.

The glint of a barrette above her right ear caught Phillip Wesley Ashcroft's eye as she turned to look up at him. With the index finger of his left hand, he ever so softly tapped the pink-and-yellow clip holding back a lock of her golden hair.

"That's a cute clip," he whispered.

"It's Hello Kitty. My daddy brought it back to me from Japan. He got a whole bunch." Her voice sounded hoarse as she spoke in a forced whisper.

"Nice."

Angela's attention went back to petting the dog. Phillip Wesley Ashcroft looked slowly across the park. *We might as well be invisible*, he thought. No one even glanced in their direction. He scanned the park left to right, person to person, slowly looking at each child playing in the sand. The adults were lost in their own world, and he realized that the time had come.

Phillip Wesley Ashcroft laid his hand softly on the left side of Angela's head, then with a quick movement, she never saw coming, slammed her chin upward and, with a powerful twist, snapped her neck. Her tiny body jerked and then went limp. Without thinking, he put his right hand on the dog's back. The sudden movement awakened Taffy from her nap. The last thing he needed was to have to chase down a stupid dog. He gently draped his left arm around Angela and pulled her into his shoulder. To any outside observer, they would look like a father and daughter sitting on a Sunday afternoon enjoying the December sun.

As he gazed out at the park, it seemed to swirl softly around the edges. His breathing was slow and deep, and he felt something much like the afterglow of sexual release. All was calm; he gently squeezed the little form beside him. She was picked at the peak of her sweetness. She would never spoil; never ferment into the bitterness of womanhood. She would remain in that state of wide-eyed expectancy of puppies, of candy in a pink jacket pocket, and the willingness to share whatever she had with a nice boy in the park. For just those few moments, Phillip Wesley Ashcroft became a boy again and, for those fleeting moments, a feminine form was kind to him.

A scream from across the park brought him out of his euphoria. A boy in a striped shirt pushed down a little dark-skinned girl and was pulling on the back of her denim jacket. Phillip Wesley Ashcroft frantically looked around the park. The nursing woman was gone. The man on the blanket was up and walking toward the boy, shouting something—the boy's name perhaps? How long had he been sitting there?

Phillip Wesley Ashcroft slipped his left arm under Angela's arm and held her firmly, his hand flat on the middle of her chest. He took a handful of the puppy's loose skin and stood. Three long strides and he was in the trees. He turned and looked back. The man from the blanket was pointing his finger at the boy and scolding him. The little girl in the denim jacket was standing next to the man, crying. All the children in the play area stood frozen, watching the scene. Phillip Wesley Ashcroft left just as he came, unnoticed.

In the daylight, the lot was not as densely wooded as he thought. Near the center, there was a clearing cluttered with construction debris and household castoffs: a couch, a broken lamp, and an old torn mattress. Somehow, he missed it in the dark. He kicked and shoved the mattress with his foot to where it lay flat, then carefully lowered Angela across it. To his left were a ditch and the exposed vent section of a large concrete drain pipe that stood about knee high. The makeshift cover flipped off easily, and he picked up a chunk of broken cement about the size of a softball and dropped it down the pipe. From far below he heard the unmistakable plop of the cement hitting water. Without a moment's hesitation, he dropped the dog and then the leash down the drainpipe and walked back to where Angela lay.

"What do I do with you now?" Phillip Wesley Ashcroft said, kneeling next to the little girl.

Briefly, Phillip Wesley Ashcroft thought of dropping the body down the drainpipe, but it seemed disrespectful. His job was to save her from becoming something ugly and evil. To cast her away as he did the puppy would take away from the beauty of what he did for her. It would have been a beautiful gesture to bury her beneath one of the trees, but he didn't prepare for that. He glanced around the lot. He must hide her, but where? Too much time was passing. The boys in the park would notice she was gone soon. He must be gone before that happened.

Phillip Wesley Ashcroft began to pace back and forth across the clearing. He was beginning to panic. It was getting harder to think clearly. Time, time was his enemy. He must make a decision. He must act. The couch caught his eye.

As he approached it, he noticed it still had all its cushions. One by one, he removed the cushions. The black lining was partially torn away, exposing the bare springs below. He quickly ripped out the black lining and rolled it in a tight ball. He shoved the ball deep into the corner of the couch's frame.

As if caressing a newborn lamb, Phillip Wesley Ashcroft lifted Angela's still body from the mattress. He held her close in his arms as he carried her to the couch. Softly and tenderly, he put her into the framework of the castaway sofa. One by one, he laid the cushions back into place. As he laid the last cushion over Angela's face, Phillip Wesley Ashcroft pressed his fingertips to his lips and blew a kiss to his little friend. The girl's small body was completely undetectable beneath the cushions.

As carefully as he could, he walked to the edge of the trees and looked out at the park. The children still ran and played in the sandy play area. The man on the blanket was gone. There were no adults in the park. He glanced at the bench. The paper bag and package of doggie treats still sat waiting for his return. With swift deliberate movement, he dashed to the bench and retrieved the only evidence of his being in the park, then returned to the cover of the trees. His eyes never left the children in the playground, and none of them looked his direction.

He quickly crossed the lot, dropping the Puppy Pretzels package into the drainpipe. He picked up the cover, placed it back on the opening, and walked out of the trees onto the street beyond. In less than a minute, he was around the corner, walking toward the bus stop.

Just like every other day in his life, he arrived, did his job, and left for home. And no one even noticed.

FOUR

Cole returned the rest of the message calls. He reviewed the drafts of three pieces on his desk and called in an order for lunch. When the mail cart intern brought him a stack of mail, he asked the teenager where to shop for a three-year-old for Christmas.

The mail kid may have been clueless but the ever-opinionated Lionel Chin offered his two cents worth: "Timeless Toys on Lincoln. Cool stuff, educational, lots of fun at Christmas. My wife always goes there for birthdays and stuff."

"Thanks, Lionel," Cole said over the top of the cubicle.

At three o'clock, Cole left for Timeless Toys. When he arrived, the store bustled with half a million soccer moms herding countless squealing, chatting, crying, and screaming kids bundled up in thick winter wear with hoods or hats. Cole was definitely out of his element. He wandered up and down the aisles for about fifteen minutes.

He knew quite clearly what he didn't want: no cars, trucks, monsters, Star Wars toys, Sesame Street anything, puzzles, games, or dinosaurs. He stood for a long time in front of a glass showcase with a beautiful doll on each well-lit, glass shelf. There were dolls of the world, baby dolls, beautiful Victorian bisque dolls, and an assortment of celebrity dolls—but nothing for a child of three.

"Lovely, aren't they?"

Cole turned to see a woman in her 60s looking into the case.

"They sure are."

"What does your daughter collect?"

"I have no idea," Cole said without thinking.

"Oh," the woman said in a judgmental tone.

"I'm shopping for my granddaughter. She's three," Cole said, for some reason trying to please the woman.

"I see. Well, these are a bit old for a three-year-old; that is unless mom is very protective and puts the dolls up on a shelf. A child has a hard time understanding a toy they can't play with."

"Good point."

The woman turned and left Cole just as lost as before. He strolled past the books, all looking very educational. He passed the blocks and things he felt were too young. Then he saw just what he wanted! Hanging on a circular rack, waited a whole zoo full of hand puppets—colorful, fun, and delightfully happy puppets. Cole picked a goofy-looking lion and slipped it on his hand. Suddenly, he transformed into Shari Lewis, twisting and turning the head, mugging like a drunk in a mirror, using his thumb and fingers to open and close the mouth.

"Hi, Jenny, my name is Loxley the Lion." Cole forgot he was standing in a toy store and took the puppet for a real test drive.

He put the lion back on the rack and picked up a toucan, a horse, and a strange opossum-kangaroo hybrid. Toward the bottom of the rack, he spotted the perfect choice: a little brown chimp. Big round eyes, wonderful ears the size of saucers that stuck straight out from its head, and best of all, the mouth formed a friendly smile with two buckteeth the size of Chiclets with a big gap between them.

"Well, hello," Cole said, picking up the chimp.

"Hello, yourself."

Cole found himself face-to-face with a woman standing on the other side of the rack.

"Uh, I was talking to the monkey here," Cole said sheepishly.

"I wasn't," the woman said with a big smile.

Cole guessed her to be about thirty-five and well worn. As she stepped from around the corner from the hand puppets, she put out her long leg, balancing it on her stiletto, knee-high, crimson boot. Above the boot, she wore a pair of very expensive, very intentionally ragged jeans and a red leather jacket that probably cost more than Cole's entire wardrobe. She stood shoulders back and chest out. She was tall and had obviously spent a lot of time in the gym. Sadly, she spent a lot of time in the tanning booth, too, and her skin was the worse for it. She tossed her dark brown hair over her shoulder and took a step toward Cole. As she did, the strong odor of cigarettes followed.

"You like to play monkey?"

Cole frowned and laid the head of the monkey across the open palm of his left hand. "Present for my granddaughter."

"Yeah, and I'm Old Mother Hubbard."

"Probably not."

"You about done in here?" she asked.

"Getting close," Cole said, returning to the menagerie on the rack.

"Almost Happy Hour. Think we might go get something to warm us up?"

"It's only 3:45," Cole said flatly.

"Okay. Well, it's Happy Hour somewhere, right?" Her cutesy voice must have gotten her a lot of drinks over the years.

"Just not in Chicago," Cole said, turning to walk toward the counter.

A kid of about sixteen, in a green vest and Santa hat, watched Cole approach. The kid's eyes darted from Cole to the woman, who now stood fists on her hips in the middle of the aisle. "Merry Christmas, Mr. Scrooge!" she called out at Cole's back.

"And to you, Mother Hubbard!" Cole said, not turning.

"Man, she's hot," the kid said, as Cole got in line.

"And therein lies the problem, son."

"I don't get it."

"Be thankful," Cole said, smiling.

The kid walked away, looking back over his shoulder at Mother Hubbard.

Back at his apartment, Cole juggled bags and packages while unsuccessfully attempting to unlock his door, and dropping his keys. Once he was finally inside, he dropped the bounty from his shopping trip onto a chair and flipped on a light. He tossed his heavy winter outerwear onto a coat rack by the door.

The second-floor apartment was not what most people would expect of Cole Sage. Though he seldom invited people over, on those occasions, he always delighted in people's reactions to the five rooms he called "home." The décor was not as dark and brooding as one might expect.

Since Cole spent most of his time alone. He spent a lot of time watching movies. He hated TV. Cole loved suspending the veil of disbelief. They weren't actors and it wasn't a story. For those 100-plus minutes, he entered another world and watched the lives of people who traveled to other worlds and took part in events he otherwise would never see. Totally submerging himself into a story, provided the great passion of his life and his only real vice.

Therefore, Cole's living room truly defined 'home theater'. On the ceiling was mounted a three-lens video projector and the wall was covered by a twelve-foot screen. His needs were few and his rent low. His money went to his passion for movies and his ever-expanding DVD collection, which recently passed the thousand-title mark.

Cole's bedroom was built for comfort. He special-ordered a bed nearly eight feet long. He was a "scooter," always ending up two feet down from the headboard, and he hated his feet hanging over the end of a bed. Total blackout curtains hid the dark film that covered the windows. Since childhood, sleeping problems had plagued Cole. His bed was soft and the sheets were silk. His pillows were three feet long and full of the softest down feathers. Cole worked hard at getting a good night's sleep.

The second bedroom acted as an office and library. There were bookcases and shelves ceiling to floor and wall to wall. CDs, DVDs, books, and even records were stored and meticulously sorted and filed. An antique oak teacher's desk took up the center of the room. On it sat Cole's computer and stacks of folders, notepads, and scraps of paper. To an outsider, it would look like mayhem, but Cole knew where every scrap and sheet lay waiting. At any time, he could reach out and grab what he needed, almost without looking.

Cole went to the kitchen, got a drink of water, and made his way to the living room. He plopped down on the sofa and kicked off his shoes. It was quite a day. He was quite pleased with himself and the Christmas presents he had purchased. Other than the occasional bottle of scotch for Brennan, Cole hadn't bought a Christmas present since his father died, nearly 18 years ago. Today, he went shopping and found just what he was looking for: a cashmere sweater for Erin, a sock puppet and a Cubbies sweatshirt for Jenny, and a first edition of *The Johnson & Wellsford Book of Anatomy*, published in 1868, for Ben. Then he remembered the call from Chuck Waddell.

Cole leaned over and grabbed the remote. With the push of a couple of buttons, Tom Waits came, piano tinkling, from the front of the room, so real you could almost hear the piano stool creak. Cole always listened to Waits or Leonard Cohen when he needed to think.

Could he move to San Francisco? In the years he had lived in Chicago, he made a lot of connections. His doorman, Sammy; Elsa, at the Norway Bakery on the corner; Phil, at the Wicker Basket market; and Louie, at the deli around the corner, all knew him by name. They never bought him a Christmas present, though. Granted, he *was* the recipient of free cinnamon rolls at the bakery and a free potato salad at the deli now and then, but those weren't like gifts; they were more like discounts or promotional items to keep him coming back. Was he being too cynical?

So, who would he leave behind that mattered? Tom Harris, Cole's best friend. But Tom had Marianne and the kids. Over the years Mick Brennan had become the nearest thing to family, but, as much as Cole hated to admit it, he'd soon be gone. Cole was very fond of Olajean but other than the few times he went to a birthday party or Fourth of July barbecue at her place, they only saw each other at work. At work, he would gratefully forget almost everyone else within a week. So why not go? Cole closed his eyes and heaved a great sigh.

FIVE

At nine fifty-one, the morning of the 20th of December, Cole flew out of O'Hare on a first class ticket to San Francisco. Two movies, eight truffles, one milk, and two Diet Cokes later, Cole touched down in San Francisco. A balding Asian man with badly tobacco-stained teeth stood at the gate holding a sign that said "Coal Stage." The man introduced himself as 'Rick' and said he would be Cole's driver while he was in town. Sitting only six feet in front of a marked police car, a shiny, black Lincoln Town car sat in a tow-away zone. Rick stowed Cole's bags in the trunk and opened the door.

"Here's my card." Rick shoved a black card with embossed silver lettering at Cole. "My number's here. You need anything, you call. Women, liquor, I'm not too happy about getting dope but I can give you a number. I know everybody, what you need, I can get. Hush, hush with me."

"Thanks, but I'll only be here tonight and tomorrow."

"Okay, I can do things fast, you just ask. Mind if I smoke?"

"Just keep the window open."

"You and me, we are going to get along. Mr. Chuck, he said to bring you to his place at 7:30. So we have to get going. Please use your seatbelt. It's the law."

The lights of San Francisco looked like the inside of a kaleidoscope through the rain-speckled windshield. Cole loved San Francisco. He clearly remembered the first time he went to the City by the Bay. In 1962, Cole and his father attended a Giants game at Candlestick Park. The Giants played the Mets and lost. He had a hot dog. The kind of frank they advertised on TV. It even had Gulden's mustard on it. His dad bought him an orange pennant and a black baseball cap with an orange 'SF' embroidered on the front. Later that day, they went to Fisherman's Wharf for dinner in a place where a guy wore lederhosen and played the accordion. To Cole's delight, they walked around the Wharf and saw a mime and an old man playing saxophone on the street. Even as a kid, Cole knew that there was something very special about this city. For a brief moment, the memory of his father saddened Cole.

When Cole left the lobby of the St. Francis Hotel, he found Rick parked at the curb, leaning on the front of the Lincoln.

"Mr. Stage! Ready to get rolling?" Rick ran up with an open umbrella. "Dinner at 7:30, just enough time."

***

Chuck Waddell and his companion of 20 years, Chris Ramos, lived in the Noe Valley district of the city. They lived in a beautiful Victorian house on a very short street. Rick double-parked and bounced out of the car, umbrella ready as he opened the door for Cole. It was six steps up to the heavy, leaded-glass doors. With a twist of the antique brass bell key, his arrival was announced, and the sound of footsteps could be heard in the hall. The form of a tall man became an out-of-focus blur on the leaded-glass doors.

The door opened and Chris Ramos stood barefooted in a skintight yellow T-shirt and a multicolored geometric print wraparound Burmese skirt. He wore a royal blue silk jacket that reached just below his ribs. On his fingers, he wore long brass fingernails at least four inches long. Chris beamed with the smile of someone obviously pleased with himself.

"Nice outfit," Cole said flatly. Over the years, Chris tried to shock, stun, and flabbergast Cole with a variety of oddball outfits, but this was the capper. Cole's job was not to react.

"You like my nong doan?"

"And that would be . . . ?"

"My skirt. You knew that."

"No, actually I didn't, but your salow is cool." Cole surprised himself by remembering the name of the blue blousy jacket.

Chris put his palms together over his head and moved his head back and forth and to and fro in his best imitation of a Burmese dancer.

"Come on in!" he shouted.

"I'll be back at 11," Rick announced, and he returned to the car.

The inside of the house was handsome. Done almost completely in Victorian-era antiques, dark woods, deep red upholstery, and thick velvet drapes. The home smelled of heavy fabric, rich leather, and money. Chris was the only child of Enrique and Anna Ramos, who died in an auto accident—but not before amassing a fortune in Texas real estate and oil. On his 21st birthday, Chris inherited $34 million dollars, more than enough to allow him to maintain his eclectic fantasies and be free of the bonds of the workaday world.

"Well, there you are!" Chuck Waddell was standing at the end of the entryway. Tall, thin, and weather-beaten, his rugged Clint Eastwood looks were a strange contrast to Chris's exotic flare for the dramatic. Chuck wore a pair of black jeans, boots, and a stiff white tuxedo shirt with the sleeves rolled up. As he crossed the room, he extended his hand to Cole and then gave him a great friendly bear hug.

"Nice place you got here," Cole said, looking around.

"All Chris's doing."

"Nice job," Cole said, turning to Chris.

"Thanks," Chris said with surprising shyness. "Hungry?"

"Starved!"

"Good! I've been bending over a hot stove all day!" Chris did his best Mae West.

"Okay, stop already!" Chuck knew if he didn't stop the campy jokes early, they would never get to any serious talk.

"A girl can't have any fun around here!" Chris stuck out his bottom lip in an exaggerated pout and scampered out of the room, his only movement from the knees down.

The dinner was remarkable. Chris truly went all out. They began with a coconut noodle soup and a ginger salad. Cole was delighted with the blazing hot, green chicken curry and crispy homemade "thousand layer bread" served with a mild potato curry dipping sauce. The main event was an enormous deep-fried catfish in a sweet red mango curry. The flavors were bold and exotic but blended for a meal to not be soon forgotten. Chris's only break from tradition was a bowl of homemade vanilla ice cream and one of the caramel fudge brownies that were Cole's favorite.

"Chris, you haven't lost your touch!" Cole said, tossing his napkin on the table.

"Let's go in the living room where we can talk," Chuck said, standing.

"You guys go on. I'll clean up and change." Chris grabbed a plate and went to the kitchen.

The living room was big and comfortable. It was a departure from the Victorian theme of the house and obviously where they spent most of their time. A large fawn-colored suede sectional sofa faced a low fireplace. Their love of books and art were apparent by the overflowing bookcases and several well-lit paintings.

"You mentioned on the phone that you had business out here. What's that about?"

Cole spent the next half-hour telling of his reconnecting with Ellie and the discovery of his daughter. Chris rejoined them about halfway through, having changed into a pair of jeans and a pale green sweatshirt with a hood. Touched by Cole's tale, Chris shed enough tears to dampen the front of his sweatshirt and several tissues. Cole explained that this was his first time meeting his son-in-law and he was nervous about making a good impression.

"Who is this guy?" Chuck said to Chris.

"A kinder gentler Cole it would seem." Chris wiped his nose one last time.

There was a lot of catching up over the next hour or so. Finally, Chuck came around to the reason for Cole's visit.

"I sort of inherited the job of staff recruitment and development for the paper. I read your piece on the elderly and the thing you did on understaffing of county hospitals. Powerful stuff, not just subject-wise but it was back to form. You got a second wind, Cole, and I want the Bay Area to be the recipient of what you can do. Out here, you'll have free reign. I have a research kid who is nothing short of amazing. He's actually the reason I thought of you. Said he met you down south at some paper he worked at, the Daily something. His name's Randy Callen, remember him?"

"Yeah, I do. Computer wizard. Nice kid. How'd you find him?"

"We didn't. He applied, and in his cover letter he listed Cole Sage of the *Chicago Sentinel* as someone he worked with."

"What a little encouragement will do!" Cole laughed.

"Anyway, I can increase your salary at the *Sentinel* by at least fifty percent. You can have your own office. You still in a cubicle? And if you press me, I might even throw in a secretary you have to share with only three other people."

"So, I come to California to dig for local and regional crap, you pay me big bucks, and we all live happily ever after. What's the catch?"

"A couple. First, all Internet rights are ours, no compensation. Second, all TV appearances must be cleared through our media department. The good news is any honorarium is yours. Look what TV did for Chris Matthews. I need you in the middle of March. My budget doesn't get approved until February reviews. I need a couple of weeks to dislodge a couple of people, and then you're in."

"Just like that?"

"Oh, yeah, and a pre-signing bonus." Chuck smiled at Chris.

"What's that?"

"You have the services of one of the city's premier apartment finders and decorators at no additional fee."

"One who has a warehouse full of goodies he's willing to loan special friends on a long-term basis."

Chris bounced his eyebrows up and down and mimed flicking a cigar like Groucho Marx.

"Sounds awfully inviting," Cole said slowly.

"Think it over and let me know in the next week or so, no rush."

"I'm in," Cole said flatly.

"Pardon?"

"I'm in," Cole said a little louder. "I would love to. I need to. I got to. I get to!" Cole smiled broadly.

"Well, all right then!" Chuck laughed. "That was easier than I thought. Hell, I was going to double your salary, I got off cheap!"

"Yeah, right," Chris chimed in.

"Tomorrow, I'll show you around the paper, and then you can have the rest of the day to look around, do some shopping or whatever. Just don't let on to anyone what this trip's about. I've just told people that an old friend was coming to town that I'd be showing around. Let's keep the element of surprise on our side."

The tour of the paper was as to be expected. In the words of Mark Twain or Horace Greeley—or maybe it was Timmy the paperboy—" If you've seen one paper, you've seen them all." They finished around noon, and on Cole's request, they drove straightaway to Tommy's Joynt on Van Ness for a bowl of buffalo stew. The sun came out, the storm was over, and the sky was a bright blue, filled with billowy clouds. At 4:15, Cole was back at SFO and on his way to Los Angeles with a new job.

SIX

As the plane touched down at LAX, a feeling of complete panic hit Cole like the back-blast of a jet. He spoke to Erin several times after Ellie's funeral. She wrote letters, sent pictures, and Cole felt they were starting to build a strong relationship. They exchanged e-mails a few times a week; mostly silly jokes and pictures, the usual clutter of cyberspace. In August, he sent Erin a birthday present. Yet, standing in the aisle waiting to deplane, it struck Cole that this was the real thing: Face-to-face interpersonal communication. He worried about the blanks, the silent spots. How would they react to the uncomfortable lulls in the conversation that were bound to come?

He gathered his carry-on and banged his way to the front of the plane, hitting at least three people still in their seats. The butterflies turned to flopping chickens in his stomach. Perhaps the two-hour drive to Erin's house would calm him down.

As he exited the gate area, Cole shifted the bag of gifts and his old leather travel bag from one hand to the other. There were throngs of people waiting for holiday visits from loved ones, and in the middle of it all stood the most adorable little girl Cole ever saw. Her face was aglow with a huge smile, and her eyes sparkled and darted from passenger to passenger in anticipation. On her feet were a pair of white high-top sneakers, and she wore blue jeans with rolled cuffs. She was wearing a sweatshirt, but Cole couldn't read it because it was hidden by the sign she was holding that said, "Grandpa."

Cole couldn't help smiling at the thought of some lucky guy getting off the plane to see a doll like her waiting for him. Then he saw Erin. She stood behind the little girl, her hands resting on the girl's shoulders. Cole walked straight to them and dropped to a crouched position in front of the little girl.

"Hi, you must be Jenny." Cole smiled.

"Are you my Grandpa?" Jenny said, nearly trembling with excitement.

"I sure am."

Jenny dropped the sign and threw both arms around Cole's neck, squeezing with all her might. Cole put his arm under her legs and swooped her to a sitting position.

"I have a puppy. It's a boy dog, my daddy wanted a girl dog, but the people only had boy dogs, but we took it anyway. His name is Buddy. Do *you* have a dog?"

"Hi, Dad," Erin said shyly.

"She is amazing!" Cole said with a broad smile. "I never imagined it would be like this. She's so big, nothing like her pictures."

"It's hard to keep up."

"We fixed up a room just for you. Daddy said it was a good thing you were coming or mommy would have never cleaned out all that crap."

"Don't say 'crap,'" Erin whispered.

"Oops on me," Jenny said, looking down.

"Shall we go?" Erin asked, with an embarrassed smile.

"Yeah, just let me get all my crap."

"Oops on Gran'pa!" Jenny squealed.

"Oh, thanks a lot." Erin laughed.

Cole just winked at her.

Within minutes of leaving the airport, Jenny was fast asleep. They missed the evening traffic, and the drive on the L.A. freeways was fairly smooth. Erin pulled into the first Starbucks she saw and bought a low-fat Caramel Macchiato for her, a venti Mocha for Cole, and a bottle of apple juice for Jenny when she woke up.

Once on the road, it was non-stop talk. There was such a comfortable familiarity between father and daughter that it was hard for Cole to believe that, six months ago, he didn't know Erin existed. They talked about work and Jenny. Erin talked with great pride in her husband's work. Ben worked as part of a pediatric research group awarded numerous honors, and whose findings were published in the *New England Journal of Medicine*, a fact that made Erin especially proud. Although she loved her work at the hospital, Erin looked forward to being able to cut back and stay at home more with Jenny.

When Jenny woke, they made a pit stop at a McDonald's for some fries and were back on the road. Armed with the French fries and apple juice, Jenny sat in the back seat happily singing and chattering to herself about what she saw out the window. An hour later, they pulled in front of a pale yellow ranch-style house at the end of a cul-de-sac.

"Look, Jenny, Daddy's home."

A tall man in dark slacks and a blue button-down shirt came out of the front door. Erin rolled Jenny's window down, which was met with squeals of delight.

"Daddy!" Jenny called from the window. "We got Gran'pa!"

The man began jumping and twirling across the lawn toward the car. The more she called out, the more he danced and bounded about, and the more she laughed with delight. Cole was sure any second he would either do a cartwheel or drop to the grass and do a somersault. This was Ben, his son-in-law. So far, so good.

Before the engine was turned off, Ben opened the door, unbelted Jenny, and lifted her from the backseat. He began to twirl with her in his arms, both of them laughing and squealing. Erin popped the trunk open and helped Cole with his bags.

"Okay, sweetie, in the house!" Ben set Jenny gently on the grass, and off she scampered. "Hello! I'm Ben." He bounded toward Cole.

Cole took Ben's hand and was pleased with the firm friendly grip.

"We're thrilled to have you with us. Please make yourself at home. We tend to be a bit informal."

"Just the way I like it. Thank you, Ben."

"You guys hungry?" Erin asked.

"Starved, what should we do?" Ben said, giving her a peck on the cheek and taking Cole's leather bag from her.

"I'm thinking the roast I have in the smoker might be a good start."

"A smoker?" Cole was pleasantly surprised.

"Oh, yeah! Wait until you taste Erin's barbecue. Wow!"

"I have a daughter that barbecues? This can't get any better!" Cole laughed.

"Yes, it can! I do beans and slaw." Ben laughed.

The three went in and were met by Jenny and her puppy. Cole was happier than he could remember. He had a family. For a brief moment, he thought of his parents and wished they could be there. If he could stop time, this would be the moment.

Ben and Erin had a warm and kid-friendly home. The evidence of having a three-year-old was everywhere, but it was a homey, happy kind of clutter. As Erin gave him the tour, she pointed out things that they did to the house and how much Ben did himself.

Erin was the queen of faux painting techniques, and several walls bore one special treatment or other. Cole was quite impressed and told her if the nursing thing didn't work out, she probably could get a job as an interior designer.

Jenny's room was a little girl's dream come true. Lots of dolls and stuffed animals inhabited the space. The theme was a kind of cartoonish Adventureland. Nothing scary, and everything looked like a bedtime story in the making. Cole thought about the sock puppet in his bag and knew it was just the thing. Under the window was a small desk with a child-sized computer and printer. On the wall was a menagerie of animals generated on the computer, but obviously colored by the three-year-old Picasso.

The master bedroom was spacious. The bed was huge and covered with pillows ready to prop up readers of the books that covered the bedside tables. Two large chairs sat next to the sliding glass door that led out to the back yard. A low table held a pair of coffee cups waiting to be taken to the kitchen. The morning paper was divided into two separate stacks. Cole was curious to see who read which sections.

Last stop was the third bedroom, used as a guest room. Ben had already put Cole's bags on the bed. This room was home to a collection of family photos, awards, mementos, and souvenirs. The first thing to catch Cole's eye was the photo Erin enlarged of her mother for the funeral. Cole still marveled at how that simple shot captured completely the girl he loved so dearly. To his surprise, on the same wall was Cole on the cover of *Chicago* magazine, matted and framed like an important document.

"You expect people to sleep with *that* staring down at them?" Cole said in a self-deprecating tone.

"Keeps 'em from staying too long," Ben said goodheartedly as he stuck his head in the door.

"Ben!" Erin said in a mock scold.

"Dinner in about 15. If you want to get freshened up, bathroom's on the right. If you need anything, just whistle!" Erin said.

Cole smiled, remembering how Ellie used the same expression and the terrible Lauren Bacall impersonation she always tried to do with it.

Erin pulled the door closed and Cole sat on the edge of the bed. "Oh, Ellie," he sighed, "you would have been so proud. How could we have been so wrong for so long?" Cole laid back and looked up at the picture of Ellie and her flowing yellow dress, closed his eyes and smiled.

He must have dozed off, because the next thing he knew, he heard the door bang open and bounce off the door stop.

"Gran'pa, Gran'pa, time to eat! Come on!" Jenny was now pulling on his arm.

Cole hopped up and followed her out of the room.

Erin set the table on the patio. The weather was warm as a spring day, just two days before Christmas. Jenny climbed up in her chair and called for Cole to sit beside her. Ben carried a glass dish filled with baked beans covered with strips of bacon. In his other hand was a big bowl of coleslaw. He set them on either side of a large platter of thinly sliced beef.

"Specialties of the house," Ben said, pointing at the bowl of dark syrupy barbecue sauce. "Top secret recipe, you know."

Erin came with a big pitcher of lemonade, and Jenny thrust out her glass.

"Not until you eat," Erin said in a kind but firm tone. "Have I forgotten anything?"

"To sit down," Ben quipped.

Erin sat and Ben took her hand, she, in turn, took one of Cole's, Jenny grabbed Cole's other and then her father's.

"For your bounty and goodness, we give you thanks, Lord. We are especially grateful for this gathering of our family and being united with Cole. Bless each one, and we pray for your safe keeping."

"Amen!" shouted Jenny.

"Amen," Cole said softly.

The food was delicious, and Cole ate until he was stuffed. The conversation flowed, and Cole and Ben found each other's conversation fast paced and interesting.

During a lull, Ben drew a deep breath and said, "Well, Erin has some news."

"Me? It's *your* news." Erin smiled.

"I've been offered a position at a children's hospital. UCSF. It is a great opportunity. It requires a move, though. That part is wonderful. Well, for me, at least. My mom lives in the Bay Area. Downside is, Erin will have to give up her job."

"No complaints here!" Erin said with a sad little smile. "No, really, I'm excited."

"I'm happy for you!" Cole beamed. "UCSF? Is that the University of California at San Francisco?"

"That's the one, the teaching hospital, actually. I'll be specializing in pediatric trauma," Ben explained.

Cole laughed out loud. "This is too much." He shook his head, a broad smile spreading across his face.

Erin and Ben looked at each other, looking for an explanation of Cole's strange reaction.

"Me, too," Cole said with a smile.

"What?" Erin said with a baffled expression.

"I've been offered a desk at the *Chronicle*. Should I take it? Is it all right?"

"All right? It's perfect!" Erin exclaimed.

"This is too much." Ben laughed. "Well, then," Ben cleared his throat and lifted his lemonade glass, "to new beginnings!"

They all clinked their glasses together and laughed. Erin reached across the table and patted Cole's hand as Ben smiled warmly at the sight of his wife and her father. He knew it hurt Erin not having family in her life. Now she was somehow more beautiful, more alive, and certainly happier than he had ever seen her.

Cole's time in California passed too quickly. The gap between Cole and Erin, that each feared would be awkward and difficult, was swept away as easily as the discarded Christmas wrappings. Her feelings toward Cole were based on stories and recollections that her mother shared. She had the advantage of a history with Cole, so in a way, she already knew him. Cole, on the other hand, was starting fresh and that was part of the fun.

Erin's resemblance to Ellie amazed Cole. Now with each hour they were together, Ellie slipped farther away and Erin came into her own. She was his daughter, his friend, and a caring, loving mother to his beautiful granddaughter, Jenny. Cole's new family filled a void in his heart, a void so filled before with the memory of Ellie that it had kept out other people and other chances for happiness.

The time Cole spent with Ellie before her death freed that space. She would always be a part of his life. Her gift was the secret she kept—the little girl she raised and nurtured. The tragedy of Ellie and Erin's estrangement was part of the healing, too. As painful as it was, without it, and Cole finding Erin, things may have turned out differently. The revelation that Cole was Erin's father was more a relief than a shock.

The sound of Erin calling him "Dad" was a tonic to Cole, and Jenny's small voice calling for her "Gran'pa" was intoxicating. Most fathers dream of a mate for their daughter from the time she's born, through the teen and dating years with the pitches and fits of terror and anger. Cole was presented a son-in-law who was everything he could ever wish for Erin. The fact that he and Ben were becoming friends was a bonus almost too good to be true.

Christmas always meant a time of loneliness for Cole. After his parents died, he always spent the holidays alone. There were the parties and get-togethers, of course, but Christmas was a time for families, and for years Cole had none. This year's Christmas was like the ones he remembered as a child: the excitement, the presents, the cookies, and the big dinner with family around a big table. This year brought back the wonderful memories of Christmases past that Cole had buried.

They all exchanged gifts on Christmas Eve morning because Ben would be on call that evening and Christmas Day. The Cub's sweatshirt Cole brought Jenny was about six sizes too big. Now that they were moving to San Francisco, maybe a Cubbies sweatshirt wasn't the best gift anyway. He took comfort in the thought of buying her one that fits at her first Giants game. But the hand puppet Cole brought for her was a big hit. With it, he was able to tell her stories at bedtime twice before he left. Cole forgot how many silly voices he could do. With the sock puppet channeling his inner child, and Jenny's laughter prompting him, he happily told stories until Erin came in to say it was time for lights out.

Ben was pleased with the anatomy book, and Cole found him thumbing through it several times. He showed Cole and Erin several color plates that illustrated arteries and nerves. Erin tried the cashmere sweater on immediately and looked lovely in it. The color was perfect, and the fit couldn't have been better.

Ben gave Cole a set of DVDs of Sixties British Bands. All of Cole's favorites singing in black-and-white and living color! Though only Cole was a fan of the music, Ben insisted they click through the chapters and sample the various bands. Cole's biggest thrill came when Erin sang along with Chad and Jeremy's "A Summer Song." Erin sang in a soft, lovely voice and knew all the lyrics. Ellie always loved "A Summer Song." Erin teared briefly as she told how her mother used to sing along whenever she heard it on the radio.

Cole started to pick up bows and discarded wrapping paper when Erin told him to sit down. "We've one more gift!" she said brightly.

Jenny struggled to pick up a package a bit too big and heavy for her, stumbled her way across the living room, and dropped it in Cole's lap. The package was wrapped in red foil and tied with wide gold metallic ribbon. As Cole unwrapped his gift, he looked up and smiled at Erin. She covered her mouth. Her eyes were moist.

"Well, what have we here?" Cole said to Jenny.

"Open it!" she squealed.

Cole gently removed the ribbons and slid his finger behind the tape. The paper revealed a burgundy scrapbook. Cole opened the cover and read the title page. "For My Father. Your Life, My Life, and the Memories I Wish We Shared. With All My Love, Erin." As Cole began to turn the pages, he was astounded to find pictures of him as a boy. On the first page was a picture of Cole and Ellie in about sixth grade standing in front of her house, down the street from his aunt and uncle. There were pictures of Ellie in junior high and high school, Cole and Ellie in college, on trips, at weddings, parties, and at the funeral of Cole's father. Along the way, Erin carefully placed tickets, notes, menus, and pressed flowers.

In the center of the book was a picture of Ellie, very pregnant, standing next to a VW Bug—they were the same shape. Cole smiled, understanding Ellie's joke perfectly. The next pictures were of Ellie holding infant Erin in a hospital bed along with a certificate bearing a little purple pair of footprints. The next pages were Erin's school pictures grade by grade, report cards, field day ribbons, student-of-the-month stickers, and an eighth-grade graduation picture. The high school pictures showed a shy girl in braces, then glasses, always standing away from the group—then suddenly, a tall thin beauty in a prom dress and then a cap and gown.

Many of the photos were just Ellie and Erin. They looked so affectionate, more like best friends than mother and daughter. The back of the book was a mix of photos and clippings of articles of Cole's, Ellie in the newspaper for some service group she was in, Erin's nursing school graduation, wedding announcement, and photos. The last facing pages were 8x10s. On the right page was a picture of Cole and Ellie standing in front of the botanical gardens in Golden Gate Park; on the left was a picture of Erin, Ben, and Jenny in front of the floral Mickey Mouse at Disneyland. The very last page was blank and in the center was a yellow Post-It note that read "Family Photo."

"I love you, Erin," Cole said with a lump in his throat.

"You like it?"

Cole couldn't answer and just nodded his head. Erin crossed the room and put her arms around his neck.

"I love you, too," she whispered.

"Where did you get all this stuff?" Cole asked.

"After momma's funeral, I went to see Ann. All of momma's stuff was boxed and in the garage. Chad disappeared, and Allen was—well, you know. Anyway, Ann gave me everything."

"That must have been rough."

"Actually, I felt sorry for her. Seems my life was a kind of weird twist on Cinderella. Ann is now just a sad, lonely girl; all alone in that big house. Allen didn't have anything, not even the house. To cover his tracks, he put it in Ann's name."

"So, the ugly stepsister got hers in the end, huh?"

"Come on, be nice. I know how it feels to not have a family. The sad thing is she has no chance of a happy ending."

"You guys ready?" Ben called from the family room door. "I'm all set!"

Erin stood, wiped her eyes, and said, "One more surprise." She took Cole's hand and pulled him from the chair. "Picture time!"

Ben set up a tripod and camera and they gathered in front of the Christmas tree, as Jenny and Buddy the dog, kicked, rolled, stumbled and chased a big colorful ball around the room.

"Okay, everybody, sit down," Ben directed.

CELLAR OF COLE

Ben fiddled with the settings on the camera and raced to join the group. After three attempts, he finally arrived before the camera clicked.

SEVEN

On his first morning back in Chicago, Cole arrived at the *Sentinel* to find his desk strewn with pink message slips, cards with candy canes taped to them, and two little gift bags with white and red tissue sticking out from the tops. He logged onto his computer and waded through dozens of holiday e-mails decorated with elves, Santas, and twinkle lights.

There were e-mails from three Nigerian princes with funds locked up in Swiss banks that needed only $1,000 to retrieve them and who'd be happy to split the fortune if he would help. There were dozens of discount Viagra and Prozac dealers north and south of the border willing to send Cole a supply of pills with just his credit card number. Altogether, there were 118 messages, eight of which were actually from people he knew and cared about.

One of the e-mails he cared about came from Mick Brennan. Cole dreaded telling Brennan of his decision to leave the paper. He had quit the paper several times, and Brennan always took him back. This time, there would be no next time.

Brennan's cancer wouldn't give him another six months. Since Cole's early 20s, Mick Brennan was a mentor, friend, and boss to him. Someone once was so bold as to call Brennan "Cole Sage's Patron Saint." Maybe they were right.

The e-mail was very short, very simple: "See me." Cole stood and clicked the mouse, closing his e-mail. He made his way to the elevator, looked down at the button, then turned and walked toward the stairs. The two flights of stairs were taken two at a time. Cole reached the stairwell door breathing deeper but not winded.

"You wanted to see me?"

"Welcome back. Good trip?" Brennan sounded tired. He leaned back in his chair and gazed at the ceiling.

"Yeah, it was nice. Erin is amazing. A lot like her mom. It's kind of weird being a grandfather, though. Ages you a bit." Cole regretted mentioning aging. Mick had lost at least twenty pounds since Cole left for California. His color was ashen, and his clothes seemed to hang on him like old drapes. The chemotherapy left only wisps of his thick grey hair. His eyes were sunken and ringed with an uncharacteristic darkness that Cole recognized as death's claim on his old friend.

"Close the door." Brennan sat up and leaned his elbows on his desk.

For a moment, Cole toyed with the idea of standing but realized Brennan had more on his mind than Cole's trip west. He took a seat in front of the desk.

"I have something to say, and I don't want to be interrupted. I want you to listen, then do what I ask. I'm not going to give you the 'we've known each other a long time' guilt trip, so relax." Brennan cleared his throat and winced at the discomfort. "Damn chemo tears the hell out of your throat. Look, here's the long and short of it. I don't have anybody. Argue if you want, but that kid of mine hasn't wanted anything to do with me in years. And divorce is divorce. You're the closest thing I have to family. As shitty as it seems, you're it." Brennan gave a soft chuckle. "I want you out of here. After I'm gone, the new guy—or, God forbid, gal—won't be... well, it'll just be different. You can do better. I know since the thing with Ellie, you've changed, returned to form, whatever you want to call it. You can do better. I'll write you letters, whatever you need. Probably nothing is necessary. You can land something easy. Get out of Chicago. For your own good, go out west, maybe. Be near the girl."

"You're going to need—"

"I don't need you looking all down in the mouth while this cancer eats up what's left of me, that's for damn sure. No thanks. Pretty Indian nurse, that's what I want to go out looking at."

"I just thought that I could be there for you." Cole felt a lump come up in his throat.

"I know, I know, and I appreciate it. Just grant me this, let me go out with some dignity, not an 80-pound slobbering morphine addict, I don't want you to see me like that. You promise?"

"Yeah, if that's what you want."

"Settled. Another thing. I don't want anybody going through my stuff when I'm gone. I've put it all in writing. It all goes to you. Burn it, bury it, shred it, sell it, give it to the Goodwill. It's all yours to do with what you will. Just keep it private. No yard sale. I don't want anybody around here ogling my stuff. Bunch of vultures is already circling my office."

"Agreed." Cole sighed in total understanding.

"Last thing. I've been squirreling away money for my retirement. Not going to make it. I'm leaving it to you. Two conditions: You said you were sending that kid you met to college. You set up something in Ellie's name? Put a chunk of mine in there to keep it going. I want you to spend the rest. Go around the world, buy a Harley, I don't know, whatever strikes your fancy. I should have done it years ago. Kept saving for a rainy day. Don't you wait, Cole." Brennan coughed deeply and opened the top drawer of his desk. "Here. I wrote this. This is all I want. It's my obit. I want it printed as is. See to it. No big bullshit flowery tribute. Bastards don't mean it anyway. Promise?"

"Promise." Cole fought back tears. He knew his friend was dying but refused to see how close he was.

"Here." Brennan pushed a business card across the top of the desk. "My lawyer. Call him. He'll fill you in on the rest. This is all too morbid. Let him earn his money."

"All right."

"What are you working on?"

"What?" Cole was surprised by the shift in direction the question took.

"You got anything started? I need a feature piece to run in the Sunday supplement. There has been too much fluff lately. I need some meat." Brennan said all he would say about his affairs. It was back to business, and Cole was relieved, but he wondered how much longer Brennan would be able to keep working.

"I'll see what I can come up with." Cole took a deep breath and rubbed the arms of the chair. "I have a couple of ideas. I'll let you know this afternoon?"

The old friends sat and talked for almost an hour about Cole's trip to Erin's, Jenny, the Christmas gifts, and Ben's new job in San Francisco. The pride Cole showed in his new family pleased Brennan. Several times, he closed his eyes and tried to picture his family when he was young and his son was a boy. Cole would think he dozed off, but then Brennan would smile and he knew he was listening. The smile he saw was at Brennan's own memories, but Cole would never know.

***

Several weeks after Cole returned to Chicago, a manila envelope arrived with an 8x10 of his family in the backyard. Cole was on the bench, Jenny on his lap, Erin with her hand on his shoulder, Ben with his arm around Erin, and Buddy the dog peeking out from behind the bench. Cole put it on the last page of the scrapbook under the clear plastic corners Erin readied for the final picture.

"Nice," Cole said to himself. And it was.

Cole approached his cubicle and could hear his phone ringing. He quickened his step and grabbed the receiver from across the desk.

"Sage."

"Cole? It's Ben."

"Anything wrong?" Cole said, feeling his heart rate speed up.

"Beware the Ides of March?" Ben laughed. "No, no, everything's fine. Everybody's great."

"All settled in? How's the new house?" Cole was relieved to find there was no emergency. He took a deep breath and slowly exhaled.

"The house is great! Erin has been breaking the bank, though, getting it decorated. Of course, my mom is helping her. I think she suffers from the 'my son's a doctor so he must be rich' syndrome." Ben laughed. "The reason I'm calling is I need to pick your brain."

"Slim pickins."

"He rode the nuke down in Dr. Strangelove, right?" The thing that Cole learned to appreciate about his son-in-law was his amazing ability to connect words, sounds, and obscure references from out of nowhere.

"Yep, he's the one 'workin' for Mel Brooks!' too." Cole offered his best Slim Pickens impersonation.

"Blazing Saddles."

"Got it."

"I have a patient." Ben's tone signaled the real reason for the call. "Little girl named Camilla. She's in pretty bad shape. How much do you know about child abuse? Erin said you're an encyclopedia of social issues and causes. I need to be pointed in the right direction."

"I fear my daughter has an inflated appreciation of what I do. What's up?"

"Camilla is the third little girl either attacked or killed in the last three months around here."

"There is a lot of abuse in the world, Ben. What makes you think there's a connection? Three deaths are tragic but not a lot to go on."

"I think there's a pattern. The pathologist who examined them is a friend of a college buddy. I met him for lunch the other day. He said the two girls died of broken necks. Snapped spinal cords, like wringing a chicken's neck. The injuries indicate a twisting motion of great force. The bones of children their size are no match for the power of an adult with adrenalin pumping. Aside from being raped, Camilla has ruptured discs, two cracked vertebrae, and torn neck ligaments. As far as the police are concerned, the attacks are random incidents that occurred in three different corners of the city. The detective I spoke with told me that every available resource has been assigned to a task force trying to head off a war between Asian and Mexican street gangs. Until they have something concrete to go on, the murders aren't a priority. Seems the mayor is more worried about damage to the tourist trade than the protection of children."

"You get to town and already you've got a soapbox," Cole chided with a smile.

"I just think there's more to this than the police are willing to admit."

"How did she survive the attack?"

"Nobody can quite figure that one out. A friend of her brothers found Camilla and brought her home. They're a poor farm people who immigrated from a tiny village in Guatemala. They're scared to death they're going to be sent home. When the father found out she was raped, he beat her. Cole, she's only eight, and he blames her for the attack! The mother brought her into the ER because of vaginal bleeding. Her other injuries were discovered on examination. The father beat her up pretty bad, but he beat her with his belt. No way he caused the neck injuries."

"Has she said anything?"

"Nothing that makes much sense. She keeps repeating "como las manos de una mujer" over and over. It means "like a woman's hands.""

"Woman's hands?" Cole repeated.

"I was wondering if you know of a database that cross-references or logs these types of cases. Maybe some patterns we could look at. I don't know, maybe I'm nuts, but I just think the cops are slacking on this one."

"How about I make a couple of calls and see what I can find out. I think I'm going to move up my timeline for moving out there, so I'll probably see you in the next couple of weeks. It would be nice to have a little down time before I jump from one frying pan into another."

"That would be great. I'd love to give you a tour of the hospital. I'm pretty proud of where I have landed."

"There's a kid at the *Chronicle* that I'll have turn up something. In case he gives you a call, his name is Randy Callen. He can get you whatever you need. I'll give my buddy Tom Harris a call, too." Cole paused, considered a thought bouncing around in his head. "Ben, what if I wrote about this? It could get the public to set a fire under the police."

"Something needs to." Ben sounded defeated.

"Best case, the police will figure out the cases are unrelated, and there won't be any more killings."

"Worst case?" Ben asked.

"We're too late to help the next little girl. We don't dwell on worst cases. You've got the ball rolling on this thing, so let's see how fast we can get some action." Cole felt that his words were shallow, and he wished he had taken longer to respond. "What kind of doctor would you be if you didn't care?"

"Is that why my mom keeps calling me Ben Casey?"

"Vince Edwards and Sam Jaffee, 1960s doctor show," Cole said, proud of his trivia effort.

"Gunga Din," Ben said stoically.

"What?"

"Sam Jaffe played Gunga Din in the movie with Cary Grant."

"That's right! How do you know this stuff?"

"Thanks, Cole, let me know what you find out." The pleasure of one-upping Cole was evident in Ben's voice.

"Yeah. Talk to you soon."

Cole set the phone down. He stood for a long moment, looking down at the mess on his desk. He looked over the tops of the grey, carpeted cubicles. Here and there, people stood talking, just heads and shoulders floating on a sea of grey. As he stood silently, taking in the scene, Cole realized how noisy the newsroom was. Phones ringing, keyboards clattering, people talking, and the whirring undertone of copy machines, printers, and computers.

His talk with Mick Brennan, followed by Ben's call, once again showed Cole how fleeting life was. He thought of the old warhorse sitting upstairs alone in his office waiting for the clock to run out on a life of words and deadlines. His thoughts shifted to a filmy shadowy figure—a fleeting image, really—a dark, unseen someone in San Francisco taking the lives of young girls. Then he thought of his granddaughter, Jenny. The little girls whose lives were ended so brutally were not much older than Jenny.

EIGHT

Cole ran his finger over the top of his Rolodex. He flipped to "H" and dialed the first number in the section. The number was answered on the second ring. "Lieutenant Harris, Homicide."

"Hey, Tom. It's Cole. Got a minute?"

"Hey, buddy, what's up?"

"My son-in-law, Ben, just called from San Francisco. They have a case at his hospital that's bothering him. Do you have any inside dope on child abuse or child murder, abductions, stuff like that that I could look at? I'm thinking of doing a feature piece on it."

"What kind of case?"

"Little girl about eight. Somebody tried to break her neck. Two other little girls have been found with their necks broken with a similar injury. Ben said it was like their heads were twisted until their necks snapped, like wringing a chicken's neck."

"Jeez."

"San Francisco PD so far isn't seeing the connection. Seems there's a big gang war brewing, and they're all tied up with that. Can't scare the tourists off. I guess the pathologist is an acquaintance of Ben's, and he claims it's the same MO on all three victims."

"Where were they found?" Harris asked.

"Not sure exactly. Different parts of the city, though."

"Sometimes we're our own worst enemy. What are those guys thinking?"

"Limited resources and pressure from on high." Cole cleared his throat. "Something else I want to talk to you about, too."

"Shoot."

"I took a job at the *Chronicle* while I was in California."

"You're kidding," Harris said in disbelief.

"Nope, start in about six weeks. You're the first to know."

"Wow, what brought that on? Stupid question. Does Erin know?"

"Oh, yeah. She's the reason—well, her and Jenny." Cole was finding it hard to tell his old friend that he was leaving. "The crazy thing is Ben took a job in San Francisco, too. I didn't even know it. Big teaching hospital."

"When are you going to tell Brennan?"

"I can't work up the guts. Would you believe he just told me I should go find a job someplace else before he dies?" Cole swallowed hard to get rid of the lump coming up.

"Seems to me that was your big chance."

"I don't know. It seems like I'm abandoning him. He has done so much for me over the years."

"Man, this is a surprise. Who will I have to abuse now?"

Cole laughed. "We've come full circle."

"Nice way to change the subject. There is an organization called—here we go—National Center for Missing and Exploited Children in Virginia. You should give them a call." Harris read off the phone number. "One of their people spoke at several department meetings a couple of years ago. They probably know more about child abuse than anybody, except maybe the FBI. They're really good about sharing, and their website is pretty good. Trouble is, this guy's M.O. is not bringing up any clear matches in the system either geographically or in the way he's killing the girls. There's just not enough data yet."

An uneasy silence prompted Cole to end the call. "Yet. Well, all right, that should get me started. Thanks for your help, Tom. I'll call you later. Maybe we can get together."

"Sounds good." Harris cleared his throat. "I'll miss you, Cole."

"Yeah," Cole said softly and hung up.

Cole ran his finger over the buttons on the phone. He was going to miss Tom Harris. They had been through a lot together. The death of Tom's first wife, Laurie, his getting shot, Cole's "dark years". They were there for each other and laughed and fought and cried together. A friendship was forged that Cole cherished. Tom Harris was perhaps the best friend Cole ever had. He'd be hard to replace.

There was no putting off telling Mick Brennan about the job in San Francisco now. He would do it after lunch. The idea for the story on child abuse would be a way into the office, and then he would tell him. Even though Brennan practically ordered him to find a new home, Cole felt a deep sense of betrayal, guilt, or maybe it was disloyalty. He needed comfort food before facing this task. He'd go around the corner to Phil's Place and have meatloaf. That always helped.

Call it a bad omen, bad luck, or bad timing, but Phil was out of meatloaf. Cole ordered a hot turkey sandwich, but it didn't do the same magic he was anticipating from the meatloaf. As he made his way back to the *Sentinel*, Cole looked around and wondered what it would be like not to walk these streets. For so many years he crisscrossed the city, chasing down leads, interviewing its people, and watching the 20-year evolution of a place where he lived but never felt at home.

Olajean Baker shot Cole a look he recognized as the precursor to an interrogation.

"Turn around, let me see the seat of yo' britches."

"What for?" Cole asked.

"The way you dragging yo' ass, I would expect to find two big ol' holes worn through. What's eatin' at you, Cole? You look awful."

Cole couldn't help laughing. The sound of this 300-pound Black charmer kicking into her Afrocentric street jive for the sole purpose of lifting his spirits never failed. The former militant revolutionary known as *Tashira* was one of the wisest and most articulate people Cole ever had known. Widely read and self-educated, she was a resource that was untapped and completely wasted at a receptionist's desk.

As far as Cole was concerned, she was as qualified and capable as anyone at the paper. Yet she chose to stay year after year, answering phones and taking messages, greeting visitors and signing the UPS log.

Of everyone in Chicago, he would miss Olajean most of all. She was part friend, part confidante, part mother-protector, and someone who he loved and who loved him unconditionally. Through all the fat and lean years they knew each other, they laughed and argued, cried and danced, and always told the truth.

"I have something to tell you," Cole began, "and it hurts worse than I thought it would."

"We ain't getting' married after all?" Olajean's wisecracking was shadowed in the realization that something was coming that she really didn't want to hear.

"I've taken a job in San Francisco, at the *Chronicle*. I leave in two weeks." Like tearing off a bandage, bad news always seemed to hurt less if it was done in one quick shot.

Olajean pursed her lips. "When did this come about?"

"When I went out at Christmas. Chuck Waddell called just before I left, and I met with him in San Francisco before I went to see Erin. He made me an offer—and I took it."

"Just like that?"

"No. Well, yes, just about. I need a change, and now that Ben and Erin have moved to San Francisco, it just seems like it was meant to be. I'll be close to them and Jenny."

"You told Brennan? He ain't gonna like it."

"I'm on my way up right now. I just felt like I needed to tell you first."

"What am I gonna do without your sorry old self in my life?"

"Maybe find that Prince Charming you've been avoiding."

"I'd have to kiss a whole swamp full of bullfrogs to find a prince big enough to handle this!" She gave a sweeping motion to introduce her girth. "Serious, now, what are you gonna tell Mr. Brennan?"

"This morning, he told me to go out and find a new job. He said things would change after he's gone and that this was my chance to make a new start. I clammed up and didn't tell him I already did. I chickened out."

"It's kind of a tightrope with him. I know you. You think you're deserting him. You can't look at it like that. Too many times, we do things thinking we're helping somebody, and they die anyway and there we are. Look what all I did for my mama. I don't begrudge her, but just the same, she died, and those 15 years are gone and ain't comin' back. When he goes, you're on your own around here. There's folk layin' for you, and you know it."

"I am going to miss you, Queen Jean." Cole reached across the reception counter and patted Olajean's cheek. She took his hand, held it to her cheek, and closed her eyes.

"I will miss you, too," Olajean said softly. "Now get out of here before I start bawlin' and ruin my new $20 eyelashes."

Cole grabbed the door handle as Olajean buzzed him through. Telling Olajean he was leaving broke down a barrier. He felt relief and finality to his decision. Telling Brennan would not be easy, but it must be done, and Olajean's reaction softened the dread.

Mick Brennan was sitting at his desk, his head down and his hand on his forehead.

"Got a minute?" Cole said, tapping lightly on the doorframe.

Brennan's head jerked up. "Yeah, sit down."

Cole approached the desk and remained standing. "Got an idea for a story I want to run by you. My son-in-law Ben called, and he has a strange case of an abused little girl. Sexually assaulted and somebody tried to wring her neck. She's in pretty bad shape—"

"What's a beat-up kid in San Francisco got to do with us?" Brennan interrupted.

"The angle was more child abuse in general. She would just be the hook. The weird thing is, there've been two other little girls murdered with the same MO. Ben thinks they're connected."

"Dr. Ben, amateur detective, huh?"

Cole didn't take the bait. Brennan's surly response would not detour him from a story that he knew would make strong copy.

"So, I think it would make a good feature piece."

"Everybody's doing child abuse stories. Everybody's got their angle. How many of these stories do you think have been written by people who've been molested?"

"I don't know, Mick. That's not the point." Cole was trying to keep in mind how sick Brennan was. The old power dance and locking horns when the editor didn't immediately take a liking to one of Cole's ideas just didn't seem to be the natural response now. The words and posturing were there, but neither of their hearts was in it.

"I just thought it was topical, timely, and has an interesting twist."

"And you're the guy to do it?"

"I am what I am." Cole did a bad Popeye impression.

"Well, what you're not, son, is a survivor, an abuse victim, someone who knows the shame and anger year after year, the nightmares, the impotence, the questioning who you are and why someone would do unspeakable things to your body." Mick Brennan stared into Cole's eyes.

"What are you saying, Mick?"

"I'll be damned if I'll go to my grave with the secret I've carried for nearly 60 years."

Cole could hear his heart pounding in his chest. He bit his bottom lip and breathed slowly through his nose. He was at a complete loss for what to say. He stood frozen looking at a man he thought he knew. For 20 years, this man lectured him, guided his career, and acted as a father figure to him—and never once did Cole have the slightest hint that he held such a dark secret.

"So, are you going to stand there staring at me like some freak in a sideshow or interview me?"

Cole scratched the side of his head, reached into the old Hershey's Cocoa can on Brennan's desk and took a pencil. He glanced around the room and saw a yellow pad on the arm of the sofa. He flipped over the top sheet on the pad and sat across from Brennan's desk.

"When was this?"

"I was eight."

"Who did it?"

"What's this, the five Ws and the H? I taught you better than that." Brennan made what should have been an ironic jest into a plea to draw him out.

Cole's mind raced. He did not want to know what was to come. This was too personal, too naked, too far inside the soul of someone he had always held as a superior being.

"Mick, I don't—"

"Don't what? You only deal with stories of people at arm's length? Strangers who you play now-you-see-them, now-you-don't with? Come on, reporter! Here's a scoop! Do it."

"Why now?"

"That's easy. I'm dying." Brennan gave a soft chuckle.

"So, we're talking the end of the war. What? About 1948?" Cole asked.

"Summer 1948."

"I know you grew up in Kansas. Were you living there?"

"Yes, but it didn't happen there. We went to see my mother's oldest sister. She and her husband lived on a small farm just outside Burlington, Iowa. My Uncle Marlin never came back from Italy. Never found a body. My dad always said he just decided to stay, so he disappeared.

"It was a great little farm, as I recall. The kind of place where a kid can run wild all day and never get into any trouble. We'd been there about a week when a cousin of my mothers showed up. He was a draft dodger. Never could stay in one place too long for fear of being caught. The war was over, though, and the threat of being caught was pretty much forgotten."

"What was his name?" Cole didn't take his eyes from his yellow pad.

"Larry. Lawrence, actually. My Aunt Ruth called him 'Lawrence.' I remember a lot of whispering in the kitchen when he first arrived. I don't think my mother was too happy to see him. Aunt Ruth seemed to like him a lot, though." Brennan cleared his throat.

"What do you remember about him?"

"He was ugly. He was tall and skinny with big crooked teeth and ears that stuck straight out from his head. He looked like he was made up of parts left over from normal people. His face and neck were covered with big deep burgundy acne welts. I remember walking past the bathroom and seeing him wearing just his undershirt and trousers. His shoulders looked like a horrible lumpy disease was eating him. I remember he was leaning over the sink and looking in the mirror. He was using a sewing needle, trying to pierce a huge acne bump in his ear lobe. He turned and looked at me and asked me if I would like to help 'pop the weasel.' I just ran off."

"Sounds like a charmer."

"That's the funny part. Years later, my mom and aunt were still joking about Larry the Lady Killer. He was always talking about the beautiful girls he went out with and how they were crazy about him. My mom and aunt always joked that they *must* have been crazy." Brennan gave a soft huff out his nose.

"How long was he there?"

"Just long enough to get the job done."

"Meaning—?"

"As I remember, when he finished with me, he was gone the next day. Could have been a day, could have been a week. I was six and was--," Brennan paused, -misused."

"How did it happen?"

"Larry said he would do work around the farm to help earn his keep. He worked, too. Cut hay, stacked wood, mended fences, pulled weeds, and whatever Ruth asked him to do. He sweats a lot. That's something else I remember. There was a river, a stream, really, at the edge of the farm. There was a bend in it that made a beautiful wide arch and created the best swimming hole you've ever seen. There was a big tree with a rope swing. I remember when I was 12, we went back, and I was allowed to go swimming with my brother and little sister. 'Safest place on earth!'

Auntie Ruth would always say when my mother raised an objection to our going alone. If she only knew."

"So, you *do* have some good memories of the farm in Iowa."

"Sure do. But it's the memory of that first summer that burns hottest, though. It lasted through two marriages, six newspapers, and it seems cancer is the only cure for it."

"Hold on. Did you say *two* marriages?" This was a second revelation, and Cole was glad he was seated.

"Had to prove I was a man. I got married at 18, right out of high school. Lasted six months. Sexual tension I didn't understand. I had a lot of hang-ups that I was too young to deal with. Took me 10 years to mellow out enough to try it again." Brennan shifted his weight in his chair.

"So, the attack occurred at the river, then?"

"That's right. It was a real hot day. Larry was mending a fence, sort of a makeshift corral really, and had just finished. I was playing inside the corral, pretending to lasso the fence posts with an old piece of rope. I remember like it was yesterday. He said, 'Hey, Mickey, you wanna go swimmin?'

"What kid would refuse a trip to the river? In those days, we all wore holes in our jeans and in summer, made cut-offs. So, no swimming trunks were required. When we got to the river, Larry stripped off his jeans and said it was 'more fun' skinny-dipping. I didn't like the idea particularly, but if that's what the grownups did, I wanted to be like them. Thought I was a big shot.

"We were having a big-time swimming around. I even got the nerve to get out and swing on the big old rope swing a couple of times and drop into the water. The second time I dropped in, Larry was waiting. He pretended to catch me. Kind of hugged me. After that, he swam up to me a couple times and kind of rubbed against me. I didn't like it but, you know, you didn't react to adults back then like we teach kids to now. Looking back, I should've got out right then and ran for the house."

"Hindsight is always 20/20. Then what happened?"

"He grabbed me from behind. I could feel him against my butt. He was aroused and rubbing against my legs. I really didn't like it. I tried to swim away, but he put his arm around my neck. I tried and tried to get free, but he wouldn't let go. His feet were touching the bottom, and he walked me to the shore.

"I remember his hand over my mouth as he laid on top of me. 'If you say a word about this, I will cut your mother's throat while you watch, then burn the house down with you, your mama, and that snotty aunt of yours in it.' I kicked and squirmed and tried to get away. Then he turned me over on my stomach and had his fun with me. When he finished, I just laid in the grass. I was afraid to get up. I knew he did something vile and wrong to my most private places, and I just laid there and cried.

"Finally, I half-crawled half-rolled into the river and rubbed myself all over. Larry sat on the bank watching me, stroking himself. I was afraid he was going to do it again, so I stayed in the water. He ordered me to get out as he pulled on his jeans.

"I could just as easily drown you as take you back. You remember what I said: One word and your mama's dead. Just for good measure, I'll do to her what I did to you. So, keep your mouth shut."

"That's all it took. The thought of that filthy animal on top of my mother kept my mouth shut until the day she died."

"You've never told anyone?" Cole said softly.

"I told my wife when our boy was eight. She asked me if—" Brennan stopped short of finishing his sentence.

"If what?" Cole asked.

"Doesn't matter. So, now you know, and I can die in peace." Brennan gave a soft chuckle.

"What happened to Larry?"

"For years, at night when I was alone in my bed, I thought I saw him peeking in my window. He was the shadow on the wall, the shape of the clothes in the closet, the sound down the hall. Then I heard my mother tell my dad that he died. I was real sad."

"Why's that?"

"Because I wanted to kill him. I promised myself I would kill him as soon as I was old enough to drive."

"Why are you telling me this now, Mick?" Cole stared at Brennan. He suddenly realized how frail and small Brennan was. Before, he only saw a sick man, a dying friend. Now, he saw a thin, ashen figure who seemed to be disappearing before his eyes.

"I've been thinking about my life. Sort of rewinding the tape and having a look. It's a weird thing knowing you're dying. Things that once seemed so important, things that changed the course of your life, are really insignificant. Things that went unnoticed or ignored are things I really want to go back and redo. This thing with Larry, I should've gone home and called my dad and told him. He would have killed him. I would have liked that. Instead, I shivered in fear and self-loathing for years."

"You were a little kid. That's why he did it. That's why threatening your mother made such a profound effect on you. Larry knew it, you know it. I want to know, though, why now?"

"I've seen you get into a story. I know how you work. You can make a difference in some little kid's life. You can warn parents that there are *Larrys* out there. The piece you're going to write will keep a little kid safe from what happened to me. You won't put my story in it, I know you well enough to know that. I also know that knowing my story, you'll work like hell to make sure you do a job that'll make a difference. Part guilt, part love, part anger, it all works for the good, and I'm gonna be dead, so I can go out knowing you did this for me."

"I need to tell you something, Mick," Cole said, standing. "I've taken a job at the *San Francisco Chronicle*. Chuck Waddell called just before I went out west for Christmas." Cole stood quietly for a moment.

"I know. Chuck called me first and asked if I objected."

"I've been getting up the nerve to tell you, and you've known all along?"

"I just wanted to see how long it would take for you to tell me." Mick Brennan smiled and gave Cole a dismissive jerk of his head.

NINE

Cole sat down on the landing between floors. The stairway was quiet and always cooler than the offices due to the slight breeze that blew up from the bottom floors. Nobody ever took the stairs, even to go just one floor. They hopped in the elevator and waited for the doors to close, rode the 14 feet, then waited again for the doors to open. As he sat in the silent stairwell, Cole's head reeled with all Brennan just unburdened. Secrets of a lifetime, secrets from a man he thought he knew as well as anyone on earth. He didn't really know him at all.

"I want you out of here," Brennan told him. He already knew Cole had taken the job in San Francisco. He toyed with him just to see him squirm.

"I just wanted to see how long it would take for you to tell me." Brennan's words made him feel like the little kid who just came clean about breaking his mother's favorite vase. Cole would be mad if he didn't already feel foolish. He spent countless hours over the past 20 years talking with Mick Brennan. They were as close as Cole got to anyone. He bared his soul to Brennan, shared the pain and grief of losing Ellie and then finding her again, only to lose her forever. All the triumphs and failures of Cole Sage's life went across a desk or restaurant table to the ears of Michael Frances Brennan.

As he sat listening to the sound of a closing door echo above him, Cole rewound the tape in his head of the "final interview" with Brennan. A marriage at eighteen just dropped into his story of being sexually assaulted as a boy, as if it were some insignificant detail. Is this what dying did to the psyche, produced a compelling desire that ensured the record was cleared?

When Ellie was dying, Cole reflected, they shared memories, dreams, fears, joys, sorrows, and confessed the most intimate desires of their hearts. That was a spiritual time, a communion of two souls separated for years trying to support and sustain each other, knowing their time together would be short. They made up for years of growing older apart. They lived a lifetime in a few precious hours and days. That wasn't Cole's relationship with Brennan. They were friends, not soul mates. Cole was the employee, Brennan the boss. But theirs was a friendship forged in mutual need for a family. For a surrogate son in Brennan's case and a father figure for Cole.

The second death within a year, of someone so close, effected him more than he allowed himself to admit. Old ghosts loomed large in his thoughts. The six months since Ellie's death was a time of sadness mellowed by sweet memories of their time together and the gift of his wonderful daughter, Erin. Cole often wondered how his reuniting with Ellie and her death would have felt if he hadn't learned about Erin.

Going instantly from lifelong bachelor to father, father-in-law, and grandfather tempered the sorrow with more joy and pride than he could've ever imagined. It was difficult to accept the changes of the last year, but Cole knew there were more changes coming.

It *was* time to leave the *Sentinel*. Cole could see all the changes Brennan warned of already taking place. As a courtesy to Brennan, the paper let him keep working. Behind the scenes, most of the work was being done—or, in many cases, redone—by the editorial staff. The woman who would fill Brennan's spot came in a month ago from a paper in St. Louis, owned by the same publisher as the *Sentinel*. To her credit, she was quietly making subtle changes and building a team, making the transition much easier than usually possible. Her respect and compassion for "Mr. Brennan" won over the lower-level staff, clerical support, and the regular staff and the column writers, which included Cole, who were referred to as "the old timers."

Doors were closing on parts of Cole's life while others were flying open—surprising and often delighting him with the possibilities. As he stood and dusted off the seat of his pants, Cole knew that the changes were good. He would miss his old friend, but in a way, it was part of a cycle and plan much bigger than Cole. Just as a seed must die to be born as a new plant, Cole Sage must shed his former self to become something new and better. If Mick's death was part of the letting go, as much as he hated to think it, Cole welcomed the change.

Three pink message slips were in the message box on Cole's cubicle wall: Olajean asking him to supper after work, Randy Callen at the *Chronicle*, and Sophie Kosciuszko. Cole dialed the number for Sophie first.

Sophie Kosciuszko was a runaway when Cole first met her. She lived on the streets, and Cole got her into a shelter and then a group home. It was a small thing to him, but she always gave Cole the credit for getting her turned around. She went to college, and of course, majored in journalism, and Cole helped her get a job at the *Sentinel*. Over the years, she came to him for advice and counsel; he became a surrogate dad or big brother, a role Cole never really warmed up to. When she married Jeff, Cole gave the bride away. He didn't really hear from her much since she quit to start a family.

Last summer, Cole went to a barbecue at their new home. Picture perfect, it sat at the end of a long drive, framed in a border of snow-white picket fencing. Their property was dotted with huge trees, shading and protecting the house and gardens from the wind. The two-story farm-style house looked like a cover for *Better Homes and Gardens*, and the Kosciuszkos looked like the subjects of a Kodak commercial. Sophie and Jeff's kids were an all-American eight-year-old boy, Aaron, and an adorable five-year-old girl, Melanie.

Jeff Kosciuszko took the inheritance left by his mother, put a down payment on the house and started a small but award-winning furniture restoration company. He worked as a lab tech after college, but the white lab coat was never a good fit. The restoration of antiques and family heirlooms was a hobby that got noticed by a local antique dealer who also was an advisor to the county museum. The hobby snowballed into more work than Jeff could do on his own. After hiring a retired shop teacher part-time, the Kosciuszkos decided that maybe they could live the dream, and Szko's Restorations was born.

On the third ring, Sophie picked up.

"So, how is my favorite ex-newspaperwoman?" Cole said cheerfully.

"Wishing she was living in Colorado." Sophie's weak attempt at a clever response signaled this was not an invitation to another barbecue.

He tried to mask the feeling, but Cole resented being used. He hadn't heard from Sophie in nearly a year and here she was in need again. It wasn't that he minded helping; it was the way she just expected him to. This was another door that, when it closed, he would breathe a sigh of relief.

"What's going on, Soph?"

"I hate to trouble you, Cole, but you're the only one I could think of who might be able to help."

"Anything you need, Sophie. You know that." Cole hoped he hadn't betrayed his true feeling in the tone of his voice.

"Thank you." Sophie took a deep breath. "It's Jeff's brother." She began to cry.

Enough with the tears already, Cole thought. The tears were for effect, and the effect didn't work on him. "Terry?" Cole asked, then waited as she regained her composure.

"He's making our lives hell. I need help to figure out what to do."

"What's the problem?"

"When Jeff's mother died, she left the family farm to Jeff and Terry with the understanding that Terry would live there. If he ever sold it, Jeff would get half the profits. She left what little money there was to Jeff because Terry would get the benefit of free rent for as long as he wanted."

"Sounds fair," Cole interjected.

"It seemed so. Jeff's mom was sick for quite a while, so she had time to think out what she wanted done. Everyone was fine with the arrangements—before she died. Afterward, it was another story."

"So, Terry wants what?"

"He wants Jeff to sign over his share of the property. We can't do it, Cole. The business is really struggling. Please don't let Jeff know I told you." Sophie's voice betrayed a well thought out, well-rehearsed speech.

When will I ever wise up to her?

"I'm no lawyer, but I don't think he can make Jeff do that if the provisions of the will stipulate it be shared only upon the sale of the property. It's clear in the will, right?"

"Our attorney says it's ironclad."

"Then—?"

"I'm afraid of him, Cole," Sophie responded.

"Afraid of him? What? Has he threatened you?" Cole was beginning to show signs of "Sophie fatigue."

"Not straight out. That I could deal with, I think. He's harassing us. He calls in the middle of the night. He doesn't say anything, but I know it's him and so does Jeff, but Jeff won't say anything. 'Wrong number,' he always says. He knows its Terry as well as I do. Terry drives by real slow, doesn't stop, just cruises back and forth. Jeff has walked out to the end of the drive, but he drives off." Sophie just kicked into bitchy mode.

"Has Jeff talked to him?"

"Yes, but he's too nice. I get so angry. Terry's his little brother, and he has always watched out for him. But this is different, *he's* different. I am really afraid, Cole."

"Okay, he drives by and calls, that's a pain, I understand, but it's hardly anything to be afraid of."

"Until today," Sophie said, her voice turning cold.

"Today?"

"I went to get the mail, and in the mailbox was a cat. The poor thing had been skinned." There was blood and God knows what all over the mail. I nearly died. Thank God our neighbor came by. He pulled it out and put it in a garbage bag he carries when he walks the dog. Oh, Cole, it was dreadful. What if the kids were with me? I don't know what I would have done." If Sophie would have thrown in a "fiddle-de-de" she would have made a perfect Scarlett O'Hara.

"And you think it was Terry's work?"

"Who else? Over the last few months since this started, we've found our dog dead and 'THIEF' written in blood on the fence boards at the entry to our driveway. Cole, we have no enemies. This is a quiet community. We watch out for each other. But no one ever sees anything."

"What is it you think I can do, Sophie?" Cole was at a loss for why she thought he could do anything. "Have you called the police?"

"Jeff would never hear of it! He says he could never call the police on his own brother. Then he'll turn around and say, 'Besides, how do we really know it's Terry?' This thing is driving a wedge between us, and I'm really afraid—"

"Well, I'll do whatever I can." Cole sighed. *Damn, she did it to me again,* he fumed.

"Can you come out to the house and talk to Jeff? He'll listen to you. He thinks a lot of you. Maybe between the two of you, I don't know, maybe come up with a plan of some kind."

"All right. When?"

"Tonight?" Sophie said tentatively.

"What time?"

"Jeff gets home around six. How about eight? I'll make that chocolate caramel dessert you like."

"I always respond well to a bribe," Cole said flatly. "See you at eight."

"Thanks, Cole, you're the best."

What kind of person would skin a cat? Cole thought as he hung up the phone. "The same kind that would kill a dog," he said aloud.

Anyone who knew Cole Sage knew he didn't like cats. And although he was not a person to keep pets, he would rather contemplate the acquisition of a dog before any form of a feline housemate. As he sat trying to imagine the terror of opening a mailbox and having a bloody, wet, skinned cat laying on your mail, he remembered as a child how he was terrorized by cats. He felt a wave of guilt for thinking badly of Sophie but still couldn't lose the "here we go again" feeling.

***

The drive to the suburbs was like a breath of fresh air. Rows of broad limbed trees and ranch-style houses lined the road as Cole made his way to the Kosciuszko's. The house was set back off the road and a large security light washed the driveway, and another on the garage covered most of the front yard.

Sophie Kosciuszko greeted Cole at the front door with a hug and a soft "thank you for coming" whispered in his ear. Jeff's greeting was hale and hearty from the kitchen where he was wiping the table where one of the kids spilled milk. The house was clean except for the hurricane of toys left across the floors and couches leading to the family room. Cole considered it a "good" mess, a lived-in, family kind of clutter that made him think of his granddaughter Jenny and her way of distributing toys throughout the house.

"Come on in." Jeff waved toward the kitchen. "The last mess of the day."

"Mommy, who's here?" came from the top of the stairs.

"You know its Cole, and you know its bedtime. So, go to sleep."

"Mind if I say hello and goodnight?" Cole offered.

"It may be the only way." Sophie sighed.

"Hey, rug rat, why aren't you asleep?" Cole growled like a big ogre at the doorway to Melanie's room.

The five-year-old gave a giggle and said, "Cause I was waiting to say 'hi'."

"Okay, so say 'hi.'"

"Hi, Uncle Cole," Melanie said cheerfully.

"Now, go to sleep!" Cole growled again in an ogre's voice as he crossed the room and tickled Melanie through the covers.

He was surprised she remembered their little game. It was almost a year since his last visit. Cole bent down and gave Melanie a peck on the top of the head and she magically pretended to fall sound asleep. At that, Cole crossed the hall to Aaron's room, where the eight-year-old awaited a more grownup greeting, and a chance to tell Cole of his latest soccer triumphs. Having gone through all the right steps of the bedtime game, Cole returned to Sophie and Jeff waiting in the kitchen.

As promised, sitting in the center of the kitchen table was a blue willow pattern plate with a tall, gooey, tear-apart baked delight Sophie called 'Monkey Bread'. There were three plates, three tall glasses, a stack of napkins, and a plastic gallon jug of milk also waiting at the table.

The three sat down and after a few minutes of the latest news on the kids, school, and the refurnishing business, Sophie reached for the jug of milk.

"Cole, we have a problem," she said, breaking the pink plastic seal on the lid of the milk jug.

"It's not so much a problem as a dilemma," Jeff interrupted.

"Call it what you will, but we need some advice, help, assistance, manpower or whatever it's going to take to solve it."

"Sophie's being a bit dramatic about this," Jeff said as Cole shot Sophie a "let him talk" look.

"All right, she told me a little bit of what's going on. Why don't you fill me in on the rest?" Cole reached over and tore a chunk off the gooey, chocolate-swirled, caramel, pull-apart bread from the center of the table.

"Look, I'm not sure you want to get involved in this," Jeff said apologetically.

"I've got a whole lot of Monkey Bread to finish off while I decide. Let 'er rip." Cole took a bite of bread.

"You kind of know my brother, Terry. He is, well, kind of different. Not what you would call a real social guy. He's taken the stuff that happened in our lives differently than I did—harder, maybe. So, I've always kind of looked out for him. Now he has made some demands that are more difficult than we're used to." Jeff paused. "He needs some counseling or something, but there's no way he'll go to get help. So, I'm at a loss as to what to do."

"Tell him what Terry is really all about. Everything. Cole is a friend, and he's not going to print the story or go out and tell the world. He needs to know what kind of person we're dealing with." There was a definiteness of intent to Sophie's words.

"It's hard, Cole. I respect you a lot, but this is very personal and hard for me to talk about. But that's not the—" Jeff paused and took a deep breath. "You see, my brother has some real issues."

"Such as?" Cole forgot how Jeff could never get to the point.

"First of all, you need to understand that my family has some real problems. Even as a kid, I sensed something was wrong. My parents slept in separate bedrooms, which I guess some people do, but in all my life, I never saw them touch each other. I don't mean mushy stuff or kissing or things like that but actually *touching*. They never did, ever. Not at Christmas, birthdays, ever. We were never hugged as children. I really believe my mother didn't want kids.

"My aunt would babysit us after school until my mother would get off work, then half the time, she wouldn't pick us up. Sometimes it would be 10 o'clock at night, and my aunt would have to call and tell her to come and get us. I know it was hard for my aunt and her family, but I think that she knew we were better off with her. Even a person with good intentions, though, can only take so much." Jeff paused before going on.

"Things really changed when I was 12. My father killed himself. Hanged himself, actually, and Terry was the one who found him. My mom sent him to the garage to get a package of hamburger out of the freezer. He found my father naked and hanging from a big orange extension cord he'd thrown over the rafters. All around his feet were porno magazines. When my mother came looking for Terry, he was looking at the magazines."

"I think I might have a few issues, too," Cole said.

"Yeah, well, after that he exhibited some pretty strange behavior. Exposing himself, drawing sexually explicit pictures, stuff like that. The school was always calling the house. The bad stuff really started when he hit high school. There was this girl. She was kind of slow."

"She was retarded, special class," Sophie interrupted. "I'm sorry, but it's true."

"Yes, she was mentally handicapped. Terry and the girl were caught in the light booth in the theatre. The girl told the principal that she would let Terry—well; he could do what he wanted because he gave her chocolate chip cookies. She said she didn't care, and he seemed to like getting 'all naked' with her. Who knows how long it had been going on. The parents pressed the matter, and he ended up in juvenile hall for six months for sexual assault. After that, it was all downhill for a while. When he was seventeen—" Jeff cleared his throat.

"Tell him. Tell him what you think happened next," Sophie pressed.

"I believe he raped my mother. It was like child molesting in reverse. I used to hear him leave her room in the middle of the night." Jeff put his hand over his eyes and paused for a long moment. "I didn't know what to do. She never said anything, but she never wanted to be left alone with him. She would ask me to stay up and watch TV with her half the night. Finally, she asked me to help her put a barrel bolt lock on the inside of her bedroom door. Not long after that, she married my stepfather, Max. She barely knew the man. She left us in the old house and moved into his. That fall I went away to school. I never went back to that house.

"When I would come home for holidays, I stayed with my mother and Max. Then when my mom got sick, Terry seemed to change. He met a nice girl named Martine, and they dated for quite a while. There was talk of them getting engaged. That ended, too."

"Tell him why," Sophie said firmly.

"She was cleaning the house and found some pictures and videos."

"What kind, Jeff?" Sophie was pushing, and Cole was getting very uncomfortable.

"They were of children doing unspeakable things. Okay, happy?" Jeff glared at Sophie. "Martine broke up with him, and he hasn't had a girlfriend since."

"Whew, he's one sick puppy. But do you think he's violent? I mean, do you think he's capable of hurting you or Sophie?" Cole stopped short of mentioning the kids.

"I'd like to think he wouldn't hurt us. He has never been allowed to see or be near Aaron and Melly. I don't know what he's into besides—" Jeff couldn't bring himself to finish his sentence. "Drugs could have brought on this demand for money, change in personality, right?"

"Certainly could," Cole answered. "So, what is the deal exactly with his demand of the farm? From what Sophie said, it sounds that your mother's wishes were pretty clear."

"Before this got so ugly, we met with our attorneys. He feels that since I got money from the estate, I should forfeit my half of the farm. I said that was silly because he gets free rent. If he wants to sell, we'll split the proceeds and that will be that. He's made it real clear he no longer wants anything thing to do with me or my family. The meeting broke up when he and his lawyer walked out.

"The last time I drove out to the farm, it was like a fortress. Razor wire and crazy keep out signs everywhere. All the out-buildings were leveled—the sheds and barn, the chicken coops, and corral for the cows. There were no animals anywhere. He even cut down the fruit trees in the garden. Everything has turned to decay."

"It was as though he wants to make it worthless," Sophie interjected.

"He has gotten a restraining order against me," Jeff said softly.

"What for, have you threatened him?"

"No. He said I was stealing things off the farm. He even accused me of selling the tractor."

"Look, I really don't understand. What can I do to help? You guys are in pretty good shape. Is the money really worth the torment? Either sign it over to Terry or you need the police to get involved."

"The police would only make things worse." Jeff held his hands up in surrender. "I would sign the stupid thing over to him and be done with it but we need the money."

"What do you mean?" Cole was surprised by the shift in the conversation.

"We have some things we could get done if we—"

"Say what you mean," Sophie snapped.

"Okay, we're broke. Happy?" Jeff shot a look at Sophie that said more than his words.

"Finally! We're broke. You said it. We need to sell that stupid farm. We need the money." Sophie stood and walked to the sink, her back to the table. Her head was bowed, and her shoulders shook.

"Look, this is a bad situation, and it can only get worse if you two start fighting each other." Cole sighed. "Jeff, do you think Terry is the one making the calls in the middle of the night?"

"Probably."

"Do you think he painted your fence?"

"Yeah."

"Killed your dog?"

There was a long pause. "I'm afraid so."

"Put the cat in the mailbox?"

Jeff nodded his head.

"Little by little, it's getting worse. I'm no expert, but you can see he's getting bolder and more cruel. You've spoken with your attorney. Can't he force a sale?"

"Not the way the will was written."

"Okay, then it's either file a police report or have somebody go talk to him." As the words passed his lips, Cole wished he hadn't said them.

Sophie returned to the table, her eyes red from tears. "That's what we were hoping *you* would do."

TEN

Cole called Chuck Waddell at the *Chronicle* before he even drank his mocha or showered the morning after meeting with Jeff and Sophie. He told Chuck his idea for a story on child abuse with the hook being the attacks on the three little girls in San Francisco. Cole suggested it be co-published by the *Chronicle* and *Sentinel* as his last and first works. Chuck agreed to look into the legal aspects but thought it could be done.

Chris Ramos, Chuck's life partner, spent days scouring the city for apartments for Cole to rent. He created a short list of possibilities, but the market was really hot at the moment, and good properties didn't stay on the market long. Before he knew it, Cole agreed to fly out to San Francisco for a long "working" weekend. It was agreed Chris would show him what he found, Cole could get some background for the story, and Chuck could get all the paperwork signed so Cole could hit the ground running when he arrived in San Francisco for good. It was decided that Cole would fly on Thursday afternoon.

The drive out to the Kosciuszko farm took nearly 90 minutes. The traffic in the city was snarled and stagnant. Cole used the gridlock to go over what he would say to Terry Kosciuszko. Plan after plan was scrapped, and it was clear that he really didn't have a clue what to do or say. A lot of his role-playing was thinking about what he could have done to get out of this in the first place.

Jeff and Sophie didn't exaggerate their description of the farm. On a road of green row crops, pastureland, and dairy cows, the Kosciuszko place was as out of place as a skyscraper would've been. At first glance, it seemed scorched and barren. A closer look revealed three ditches to nowhere. Deep piles of soil ran along what must have been trenching three to four feet deep. The buildings that Jeff said were torn down, lay in the rubble where they stood. A smaller outbuilding, that looked like some of the dairy buildings he passed, was totally demolished. The Caterpillar tractor was still parked with its front wheels on top of the ruins it had knocked down.

In the center of the brown piles of soil and acres of dry golden grass sat the house. There were no shrubs or trees in the yard. There was no lawn or landscaping of any kind. It could have been dropped there from any late '60s subdivision in America—a wide ranch-style house with red brick trim, shingle roof, and a big white garage door. The difference was it looked dead.

The fence across the front of the farm was part chain link and part hog wire. Looped across the top of the fencing was a single strand of razor wire. The image of hog wire topped with the vicious spikes of the razor wire was hard to process. Who was its intended target? The gate at the front of the property was closed and, oddly enough, a padlock dangled at the end of a chain that suggested it was locked most of the time. It didn't take much effort to push the gate open. Cole left it open, just in case he needed to make a hasty exit, and drove up to the house.

Chicago is full of abandoned buildings more welcoming than this place, Cole thought as he approached the front door. He took a deep breath and rapped on the door. Next to the door, the wires for a doorbell poked from the wall. Cole knocked a second time, only a bit harder. A minute passed. Cole breathed a sigh of relief and was about to return to the car when he heard the sound of a motor. Turning, he saw a dusty green Ford pickup approaching the house.

"Who the hell are you?" shouted the morbidly obese, red-faced man that Cole barely recognized as Terry Kosciuszko.

"How ya doin', Terry? Cole Sage. Remember me? I'm a friend of Jeff's."

It was hard to believe the man coming around to the front of the truck was the same man Cole met at Jeff and Sophie's housewarming three years before. He looked like he weighed close to 300 pounds, and his face was the color of a tomato. The T-shirt he wore was stretched so tight, it was nearly see-through. He wore a pair of cargo shorts, so filthy their original color was hard to detect. Terry's feet were a shade of deep burgundy and overran the flip-flops so badly that only the straps were visible. The skin on his legs was covered with psoriasis and swollen to the point it looked like they would split open.

"I don't want any," Terry barked out.

"I haven't got any," Cole said calmly.

"What do you want?"

"Have a little talk."

"Why?" Terry now stood just a few feet from Cole.

"Jeff and Sophie are concerned about you."

"Like hell they are."

"You'd be surprised. Can we sit down or something?"

"No," Terry said emphatically. "My business is none of yours."

"That's funny," Cole countered.

"What's funny?"

"That's what I told Jeff and Sophie. What you do is none of my business. But they asked me to talk to you anyway. They thought a third party in the situation, who wasn't a lawyer, might be able to straighten things out."

"Like I said, it's none of your business."

"How long have you lived here?" Cole asked, ignoring Terry's hostile tone.

"All my life."

"Wish I could have seen it before. Maybe I could appreciate the changes you've made."

"What are you, some kind of smart-ass comedian?"

Cole was momentarily distracted by the rattling caw of a crow.

"It is just strange to me that someone who wants something bad enough to skin a cat wouldn't take better care of it."

"You're on my land, and I could shoot you for a trespasser," Terry said as white foamy saliva gathered in the corners of his mouth.

"Nope. Still murder. I'm here at the request of the 50% owner of this farm. Invited people aren't trespassing. So, why don't you drop the tough guy act and tell me what you think the problem is."

"There is no problem. My mother left the place to me," Terry said.

"Then why should Jeff sign over his share if it's already yours?" Cole replied, surprised at Terry's argument.

"He tricked her."

"And her lawyer?"

"They don't like the way I live."

"I must admit it is a bit barren out here."

"What are you into, Mr. Sage?" Terry's tone softened.

"How do you mean?" Cole felt the conversation taking a turn he was not prepared for.

"I like little kids." Terry leered at Cole and then broke into a big grin.

Cole tried not to change expressions or react. "I heard you have peculiar tastes."

"It makes me feel good. It makes me money, lots of money and friends. I have friends all over the world who share my 'peculiar tastes,' as you call it. You are so hung up with your Anglo-Puritan restraints that you have probably never even talked with a friend about *your* sexual preferences." Terry laughed. "You don't know whether to smile, shit, or hit me."

"Is this the kind of thing you try on Sophie for shock value?" Cole replied, unfazed by Terry's perverse attempt at intimidation.

"That frigid bitch is the reason my brother won't give me what's mine. Someday, I'll give her what she really needs." Terry grabbed his crotch with his fat hand.

"She's not a child. She would probably laugh at you. Look, you don't shock me. I think you are a fat, disgusting pervert. Here's the deal. Your brother won't bring the police into this, but I will. I want you to leave them alone. Don't call them. Don't drive by their house, and enough with the animals. I am not a violent person. But there is something about you that makes me understand why people are beaten with baseball bats. I don't condone it, but I am beginning to understand it. Do I make myself clear?

"Are you threatening me?" Terry said in disbelief.

"Are you wearing a wire?" Cole smirked. "Yes, I am, as a matter of fact. No, that's not right, either. I'm promising you."

"I'm not afraid of you. You don't know me. I can make your life miserable."

"I can see what you've done with yours." Cole smiled. "Looks like you're pretty good at it."

"We'll see who has the last laugh." The look in Terry's eyes was pure evil. As he moved toward Cole,

Cole could smell the stench of the bloated mass before him.

"Just remember what I said," Cole said, moving toward his car.

"Don't forget to write." Terry laughed and turned to go into the house.

ELEVEN

A crush of people with digital cameras around their necks and Alcatraz sweatshirts on their backs exited a blue-and-gold tour bus and flooded Bush Street a block from Chinatown's Dragon Gate, taking Phillip Wesley Ashcroft along with them. In his Giants sweatshirt and cap, he would have fit right in, except for the fact that he wasn't Japanese.

Grant Street's swirl of colorful sights and symbols, exotic smells, and sounds of clanging gongs and Chinese music blasting from every third door just got tourists' wallets itching. It also would make it easy for Ashcroft to spirit away a little girl with jet-black hair and beautiful almond eyes.

For the third day this week, he took a late lunch. Not that anyone would notice. He hopped a Muni bus to Market and Powell and walked the six blocks to the Chinatown gate. The first day, he was too late and the second, he saw just the last few stragglers making their way home to the apartments above the many shops and restaurants. On his second visit, he found an alley off a side street that would afford him a clear view of anyone coming along the sidewalk and where he could wait in the shadows unnoticed.

Today, his timing was perfect. Kids were everywhere shouting, laughing, squealing, and swinging their Hannah Montana and SpongeBob backpacks at each other. Ashcroft made his way to the alley and stood behind a dumpster. He tried to take deep, slow breaths. He was so excited this time. He knew there would be children, so many children. He felt like a housewife at a Macy's bargain basement sale. He envisioned what he wanted, but he feared she might not come along this street.

As he waited, he thought how the game had changed, how he had refined it. Mostly, he thought of how easy it was. The release, the gratification, built with each precious new friend. He longed for the nearly blinding blast of white light in his head, the feeling of nearly floating, and the total relaxation of every muscle. He longed to make his way back to work suspended in the soft cloud of tenderness and protection he felt for the one he would be saving. Who would she be?

There was no need to make love to her. It didn't work before. Touching his little friend that way was not right and certainly was not what he was supposed to do. He knew it now. The pure release and thrill of fixing them in time and stopping their descent into the callowness of womanhood were more than he could have hoped for. He learned so much and had done so well. It would only get better from here.

The alley was deep in shade from the buildings around it. As far as Ashcroft could tell, there was only one doorway into the alley on each side. At the end, a chain link fence stood atop a three-foot brick wall. Three dumpsters lined each side of the alley. Next to the door on his left were six plastic milk crates filled with bottles of an unidentifiable dark, oily liquid. Just above the door to his right, an oversized yellow light bulb glowed just enough to show that it was on. Phillip Wesley Ashcroft turned his attention back to the street at the sound of footsteps.

Another perfect little friend was about to enter his life, a small Chinese girl with a pink Barbie lunch bag. She was walking along, intentionally scuffing her feet on the sidewalk. As she approached a soda can, she did a skip step and gave it a goal-worthy kick. The can bounced along ahead of her, and her arms shot straight into the air as she shook her head triumphantly from side to side. A broad smile crossed her face, and Phillip Wesley Ashcroft knew he had found the one.

The last 20 feet to the alley seemed to take forever. She stopped, she twirled, she played a free form kind of hopscotch, and Ashcroft's breathing became shallow and rapid. He felt hot and sweaty. She needed to get here, she needed to hear his story, she needed to understand why he needed to save her, now. Six feet away... three... She hopped off the curb and into the alley entrance. Ashcroft stepped in front of her and smiled.

"Have you seen my kitty?" he asked sadly. "She jumped from my arms, and I think she ran down this way. I was taking her home for my little girl."

The little girl shook her head cautiously.

"Do you have a kitten?"

"A big cat."

"My little girl Amber wants a pet so bad. You're lucky. Will you help me find her kitty?" A hint of pleading in Ashcroft's voice made him sound friendly, even a bit needy. He watched as she processed his words and remembered the rules about not talking to strangers. Her eyes flicked about the alley and back to his face. He won, she would help; the sweetness of childhood won over the cynicism of the adult world that would suppress her natural desire to be helpful.

"I'm supposed to go straight home."

"With your help, it will only take a minute. Amber will be so happy."

"Well, okay, but just for a minute."

"Oh, thank you! I think I heard it meowing down there." He started toward the big green dumpster on the left side of the alley. "What's your name?"

"Lucy," she said, following Ashcroft into the alley.

Without Lucy noticing, Ashcroft let her get in front of him. He bent down and called to the fictitious kitten.

"Here, kitty. Here, kitty," Lucy called as she looked behind bins and dumpsters.

There was a short concrete block wall on the right side of the alley that shielded a dumpster from view. As they reached it, Ashcroft swept his arm around Lucy's waist and clasped his hand down hard across her mouth. With one swift direct movement, he stepped behind the block wall and seated himself, Lucy on his lap, on an overturned milk crate.

"I want to tell you a story," he whispered into the little girl's ear. She wiggled and kicked and struggled against his grip, but it was pointless. "Be still and listen. I want you to understand. I'll not hold you so tight if you promise to be still."

Muffled words and a shake of her head brought Lucy's struggling to an end.

"This won't take long. But you need to hear my story. Then I'll be gone. Are you ready?"

Lucy nodded her head. Tears streamed down her cheeks, and Phillip Wesley Ashcroft could feel them on his hand as he began. "When I was a student at the university, I met an Asian girl just like you. She was from Hong Kong. Her family owned a restaurant that I ate at quite often. She was very pretty and would bring me my water and a menu each time I came to the restaurant.

"It took a lot of courage, but one day I asked her to go to the movies with me. She said she had to work. I asked her to go to a play at the university. She said she had to take her mother somewhere. I thought she was telling the truth. She seemed like a very sweet girl. The next time I went, I asked her out again. She had an excuse. Each time I went to the restaurant, I would ask her to go out. I took her flowers, candy, and once I tried to give her tickets to a university basketball game. She said she did not want to go out with me.

Ashcroft shifted the weight of the little girl.

"I thought she liked me and I told her so. She said not to ask again. I was very sad. I called the restaurant and tried to talk to her, but whoever answered always said she was busy. I went to the restaurant with flowers and decided to try once more. They said she was not there. I left the flowers for her." Lucy seemed to relax a little, interested in the story.

"As I passed an alley on the way back to school, four Chinese boys stepped out of the dark and told me to leave their sister alone. I tried to tell them I liked their sister very much, but they wouldn't listen. The next thing I knew, they were hitting me with wooden sticks and punching and kicking me. I woke up all bloody and hurting. It was the middle of the night, and I was in the alley, all covered with garbage.

"I'm not a bad person. She should have gone out with me. You are Chinese like her, and you were willing to help me. You are sweet and kind. I am going to help you now. You must stay the sweet girl you are forever. Thank you for your sweetness."

Ashcroft tightened his grip on the tiny girl's mouth and slipped his arm up under her chin. With one quick, hard, twisting jerk, he broke her neck. She lay limp on his lap. He sat for a moment, gently rocking and humming. The release was pure white light, and he felt as if he was floating, but the warmth of the afterglow was interrupted by spreading wetness on his leg. The little girl's bladder emptied.

"You've ruined it!" he growled. "Just like her. You are all alike." Phillip Wesley Ashcroft stood and looked about him.

He tried to hold the dripping child away from him as he lifted the black plastic dumpster lid. He squeezed the dead child by the back of the neck and grabbed at her feet. With a clumsy grunt, he hoisted her body up and into the dumpster. He fumbled for the lid and slammed it down on the little girl lying atop the black plastic garbage bags.

Phillip Wesley Ashcroft looked down at his wet trousers and cursed under his breath. "I look like I pissed myself," he growled as he left the alley.

***

The flight from Chicago was rough. A storm over the Rockies forced the flight attendants to strap in and have barf bags at the ready. As he stood in the cool San Francisco wind, Cole breathed deeply and tried to shake off the fading motion sickness. In the taxi, he rolled down the window and let the crisp air revive him. By the time he reached the *Chronicle*, he was 100 percent.

His initial meeting with Chuck Waddell was brief. They agreed to meet in a couple of hours to go over the details of Cole's story idea. They would tie up some loose ends regarding office space, Cole's preference for a computer, and an idea Chuck floated for a syndicated column.

"Check in with personnel," Chuck said. "Look for Beth Swann, she'll have all your paperwork."

A half dozen people suddenly burst into Chuck's office with arms full of files and notepads.

CELLAR OF COLE

Cole gave Chuck a wave and was off to find personnel.

Like all good plans, the woman he was looking for was, of course, out of the office for an hour. Cole decided not to wait and asked to use a phone. He reached Ben's cell phone, and they agreed to meet at Pearl's Burgers on Post Street in 15 minutes.

Pearl's was the stuff legends are made of; fat burgers, great fries, and easy to pass up if you didn't know where you were going. Cole didn't and drove by twice before he spotted it. Inside, there were only six tables, and seated at the one farthest from the door was Ben and a tall Asian man in a black leather sports coat.

Seeing Cole, Ben jumped to his feet and made his way through the lunch crowd with a big smile and his hand extended.

"What's up, Doc?" Cole said, pleased at the warm welcome.

"You're looking well!" Ben began. "We have a table over here."

The pair made their way to the table, and Ben introduced the man. "Cole, this is Lt. Leonard Chin of the San Francisco PD. Len, this is my father-in-law, Cole Sage, formerly of the *Chicago Sentinel* and newly of our own *San Francisco Chronicle*."

"My pleasure," Chin said, shaking Cole's hand.

"Sorry I'm late. I kind of passed it up a couple of times." Cole shrugged.

"Happens all the time, but it's worth the effort. I'm on a time thing, so I ordered for you. I hope you don't mind." Ben smiled.

"Gives new meaning to 'just what the doctor ordered,'" Chin quipped.

"I asked Len to join us because he has been assigned to the Lucy Zhang case."

"Lucy Zhang?" Cole didn't recognize the name.

"I guess you haven't heard. We have our fourth victim. She was found in a dumpster in an alley in Chinatown last night. Neck broken, just like the others." Chin was no longer smiling.

Cole looked from Ben to the policeman. "Are we any closer to having a suspect?"

"We've got one little girl in the hospital. If we could only get her to talk, she could give an eyewitness description. She just keeps babbling about women's hands." Chin shook his head. "I tell you what, I have about 500 Chinese gangbangers who would love to make this a race issue, gang issue, or any other kind of issue. Any excuse to start shooting. This could get real ugly."

"What are the odds of that?" Ben asked.

"Million to one. Mexicans don't fit the profile. Neither do blacks. We're looking for a white guy, mid-to-late 30s, single, a social outcast. Probably works in computers or some other job where he spends all his time alone. How many of those you think we got in a 10-mile radius?"

"There's no physical evidence? No DNA? Nothing?" Cole pressed.

"Our guys say Lucy wet her pants either during or moments after the killing. There was no urine on the bags she was lying on in the dumpster. That means the killer probably got wet. So, yeah, we have DNA, but it's going the wrong direction at the moment." Chin paused. "Ben says you're doing a story on this case."

"That's right." Cole nodded. "We need to start connecting the dots somehow. There has to be a link to the four little girls," he added.

"I need a favor. I want you to say that we have a witness. Someone who saw him leave the alley."

"I can't do that."

"Why not?" Chin said in disbelief.

"It's not true," Cole said firmly.

"It could very well flush him out. If you say it, the TV people will pick up on it, and it'll be everywhere."

"Exactly. I won't do it. I will quote you, though."

"How's that?"

"If you say you have a witness, I'll quote you. The lie's on you, not me. I'll help you any way I can, but I won't intentionally lie to my readers. If it comes out that there's no witness, you lied, not me."

"A fine line, Mr. Cole."

"Maybe, but that's how I work."

"Done. I have an eyewitness that saw a white male in his mid-to-late 30s leaving the alley. Quote me if you want. Or use that 'a high-ranking source within the SFPD thing that you guys always use. Whatever way you want to do it." Chin knocked on the table with his knuckle.

"All right. I have a meeting with my editor in an hour. I'll pitch him the story. I'm kind of walking a fine line here. Chicago is still home for two weeks. Officially, I don't start at the *Chronicle* for three, but I'm pretty sure we can get this done."

Their talk was interrupted by the arrival of a young woman with a tray piled high with burgers and fries. Lt. Chin ate silently while Ben and Cole tried to outdo each other on the list of movies they'd seen recently. Cole conceded that Ben won when he told him of finding *Head Over Heels* on an Internet movie site. Long a favorite of Cole's, Ben could now brag of having seen both versions of the film under both titles: *Head over Heels* and the re-edited release under the title *Chilly Scenes of Winter*. They agreed that after dinner if Erin and Jenny would let them, they would watch the two endings of *Chilly Scenes of Winter* and decide which one was really the best. Ben grabbed the check when it came.

"Isn't that a form of graft?" Cole teased Lt. Chin.

"Only if I asked for extra bacon," Chin quipped.

"Policemen don't eat bacon; it's cannibalism," Ben said, moving to the counter.

"Ouch." Chin laughed as he reached into his jacket pocket for a business card. "If you need more background, give me a call." Chin headed for the door.

"Thanks." Cole slipped the card into his shirt pocket. "See you tonight, Ben." Cole waved.

"Welcome to San Francisco," Chin called while Cole stepped outside.

When Cole arrived back at the *Chronicle*, Beth Swann returned from lunch and was holding court at her cubicle. In his younger days, he would probably have been one of her swarm of admirers. She was tall, blonde, and all legs, eyes, and pearly white teeth. Her hair fell across her shoulders like a spun gold waterfall. She was simply beautiful.

The thing about Beth Swann that struck Cole, though, was her voice. As she laughed, flirted, and teased the three young men around her, her voice was deeper than he expected. Not harsh or husky in any way, but a sexy velvet timbre—an octave lower than someone her age and with her sun-kissed looks might have. Just like Renee Zellweger's character said in Jerry Maguire, she had Cole at "hello."

"I was told to see you about my hiring papers."

"And who might you be?"

Cole thought of a dozen snappy retorts. He caught himself and accepted the fact that Beth Swann was as far out of his league as she was for the three stooges who had just scurried back to their cubicles. "Cole Sage," he said with a restrained smile.

"A man who knows who he is. How refreshing." Beth cocked her head to one side and frowned. "*Chicago Sentinel*, right?"

"That's right." Cole was amazed she knew who he was.

"A friend sent me the piece you did on mental health and seniors. Really touching. Nice to meet you, Mr. Sage. You'll be a nice addition to the *Chron*." Beth extended her hand.

As Cole took her hand, he saw in her eyes an intelligence he wasn't expecting. He was a bit chagrined at the totally sexist first impression and judgment he had made.

"Thanks. I think it's going to be a good fit."

"When you get settled in, maybe we could have lunch sometime. I'd love to talk to you about writing. I have a degree in journalism from UC San Diego, for all the good it's doing me. Maybe you could give me some tips on how to get out of this dungeon and out on the street." Beth smiled wide. "In a good way, I mean."

"I would be delighted." Cole suddenly felt old and instructional.

It took about 15 minutes to go over the hiring package, fill out and sign a ream of paperwork.

"Okay," Beth finally said, "that should just about do it. There is one more thing we need to do, but I'm not good at the retirement options stuff, so if you don't mind, I'll have someone else go over those with you. He's at lunch right now, so maybe you can catch him later. No rush on those. If you don't have time today, you can see him tomorrow." Beth gave Cole a dazzling smile and said, "I am really glad I got to meet you. Welcome to the *Chronicle*."

Cole stood and took copies of the multiple documents he had signed. "I'm sure it'll be wonderful.

I look forward to our lunch. By the way, what's the name of the person about the retirement stuff?"

"Phillip Ashcroft. He sits right over there."

TWELVE

Cole tapped his pencil impatiently as the phone rang for the twelfth time.
"San Francisco Police. How may I direct your call?"
"Lieutenant Chin, please."
"One moment," the robotic voice replied.
Three rings and a buzz later, "Chin."
"Cole Sage here. Got that list for me?"
"Sure do. Got a pencil? I'd fax it over to you but I've never learned how the damned thing works."
Leonard Chin proved to be a valuable resource. With his help, Cole hit the ground running. He provided Cole with dozens of leads, names, and contacts that someone new to the city would have taken weeks, even months, to develop.
"That's going to be a great help. I owe you."
"Hey, one other thing. I talked to the Zhang's and they are willing to talk to you later today if you have the time. I told them three, but I'll give you their number if you need to reschedule."
"No, that's great," Cole said. "You have been a great help."
"No luck with the Luis's though. The old man has disappeared and the wife is too freaked out to talk to anybody."

"How's the little girl?" Cole asked.

"Still pretty out of it. Just babbles in her sleep. Just bits and pieces in Spanish."

"Well, we take what we can get, huh?"

"Name of the game. Talk to you later."

With only a week left to prepare for his move, Cole could make valuable headway on his story thanks to Leonard Chin.

Chris Ramos called a few minutes later. He made appointments for Cole to see several flats and apartments. They spent the entire morning running up and down stairs and walking through echoing empty spaces. Cole felt that any one of them would be an improvement over his place in Chicago.

At noon they stopped for lunch at a small, dark, Italian restaurant called 'Mama's Kitchen' tucked back in a neighborhood with no parking. Chris was welcomed with open arms by the owner, Tommy Caravallo, and made it clear that one, they were starving and, two, that Cole was not gay. The conversation quickly turned to the real estate business, and Chris's desire to find something for Cole perfect and cheap. Tommy stopped the conversation and ran to a phone next to the kitchen door.

"I got it, just what you want," Tommy said dialing the phone.

"That's what *he* said," vamped Chris.

The big Italian rolled his eyes. "Swing by the funeral parlor on 24th Street and pick up the key. Lease option, $1,200 a month, and it applies to the purchase price. They only want 500 thou'. It's a steal, belonged to my partner Billy's uncle, he died last month and they just want to be rid of it."

"Where is it?" Chris inquired.

"It's a surprise—but, girlfriend, take along nitro pills and an oxygen tank 'cause you're going to have heart failure when you see it." Cole took a double-take at the burly Italian in the white shirt and apron. When he finished speaking to Chris, he winked at Cole.

"Gay?" Cole whispered as they made their way to a table near a window.

"We're not all as pretty as me," Chris smirked.

The house was beyond Cole's wildest dreams; tucked one street back from the marina, the two-bedroom home stood proudly among the larger homes and converted apartments. Four thick concrete steps opened onto a covered porch the width of the house. The massive dark oak door framed thick leaded stained glass that pictured a seagull in flight in an azure blue sky with the sun on the right and moon on the left. At the bottom, waves of blue-green broke on a shore with two tall redwoods.

The door opened to an entryway of hardwood floors, shelves, and trim—all of quarter-sawn oak. Throughout the house, mission-style woodwork brought continuous whistles, wows, and ahhs from Cole. In every room, there were pieces of rich antique mission-style furniture: tiger oak mantels graced two fireplaces, and a huge round oak table sat in the center of the dining room.

The living room was dark and a foot-deep shelf ran around the top of three walls about 18 inches below the ceiling. A fireplace with a pillared oak mantel graced the back wall and was framed in floor-to-ceiling bookcases. It didn't take long for Cole to mentally place his big-screen television and surround sound speakers. This was the kind of room he always dreamed of. Two bedrooms set off the large, square living room.

"So, you think this might be the one?" Chris said with a big smile, leaning against the archway into the living room.

"Forget the lease; I'll buy it. What do we have to do to make sure it doesn't get away?"

Chris flipped open his cell phone and hit a button. "Bobby, Chris. Sold, if the furniture stays." A pause, then he chipped, "Me too. Who's gonna do the paperwork?" There was a long pause and Chris said, "Got it. Love Ya. Peace."

"Bobby said the furniture is too butch for his taste and you're welcome to it. Silly boy." Chris gave Cole a thumbs-up. "So, it's all yours, big fella. Pacific Title will do the paperwork. My friend Kim works there; he'll take real good care of you."

"Anywhere you *don't* have a friend working?"

"Hooters." Chris threw his head back and laughed.

Chris arranged for the papers to be drawn up and set an appointment for Cole to meet with Kim at 11 o'clock the next day. The next stop for Cole was not as pleasant.

The Zhang's lived in a large apartment above the herb and dried foods store they owned. The weight of sadness hung in the apartment like a heavy fog. The strong odor of incense filled the living room where they sat across from a shrine covered in flowers, candles, and photographs of Lucy. An odd mixture of Chinese icons and pictures next to statues of Catholic saints filled the home.

Mrs. Zhang never spoke but sat softly weeping and dabbing her eyes with a pale pink handkerchief. Mr. Zhang spoke in hushed tones, but it did not hide the anger and frustration he felt toward the police and their inability to find his daughter's killer. Cole tried to assure them that he would do everything possible to bring public pressure on the police to focus on this case and force them to reexamine the connections among the other children's deaths.

Cole quickly realized that the interview would not yield much. Most of his questions were answered in short two- or three-word phrases. Except for Mr. Zhang's bursts of criticism of the police, his responses signaled his unwillingness to share what was in his heart.

It was apparent the thing that sustained the Zhang's was their faith and the comforting words of their priest. After 25 minutes, Cole left the apartment deeply touched by the Zhang's loss, with few notes and fewer answers to why the killer would have chosen the lovely dark-haired little girl with the bright smile.

As Cole sat staring at the wall in his makeshift office, he twisted the plastic lid from his mocha one too many times, and the crackle as it snapped in half brought him back from his thoughts. The meeting with the Zhang family left him drained and reflective. He was impressed with how their faith sustained them through their unthinkable loss. The soul-deep pain thrust upon them was tempered by their belief in knowing they would see Lucy again in heaven. They referred to their pastor, Father John, frequently, and drew on his words of comfort and teaching to get them through the nightmare of Lucy's murder.

THIRTEEN

The call to St. Ignatius parish hall disappointed Cole. Father John had gone to a meeting across town, and wouldn't be back in the office until the next day. As almost an afterthought, the secretary did mention, however, that he would be back in time for his support group that very evening.

"Support group?"

"Adult child abuse group," the secretary said softly.

"Is anyone welcome?" Cole asked.

"Everyone is welcome in the house of God, Mr. Cole."

Cole felt foolish. He asked the time and location of the meeting, thanked the secretary, and got off the line.

Traffic was backed up for blocks, and the crew working on the street was in no particular hurry to go home as Cole slowly rolled by the hole the power company had dug in the middle of Grant Street. St. Ignatius was a little church on the edge of Chinatown that served the Chinese community as well as the neighborhoods to the northwest. Cole drove by the little grey church the first time; it was tucked back between two large nondescript buildings, and Cole was expecting something far grander and ornate.

CELLAR OF COLE

The little iron gate on the left side of the church was just as the secretary described. Cole was nearly 15 minutes late as he entered the long hall that led to the Fireside Room. Thankfully, the door was open and Cole slipped unnoticed into the meeting.

There were 10 people sitting in a semicircle facing a tall, thin man who stood behind a small table. Cole was trying to decide which empty chair to sit in when the man looked up with a friendly smile and waved Cole forward to a seat on his left.

"Terri called and said she would not be with us tonight. So, sorry to say, there will be no goodies. But don't despair; she said next week, she'll bring double. So, Carl, you can't get your fill of those caramel bars she makes until next time."

The group gave a knowing laugh, and all eyes went to a pudgy little man with a big smile and red face sitting opposite Cole.

"Welcome to our group," the tall man said to Cole. "I'm Father John, and we were just about to introduce ourselves."

"Sorry I'm late," Cole said as he sat down. "My name is Cole."

"Welcome, Cole, we're glad you came." Father John turned to the first seat and smiled.

"I'm Kari, and I love dogs," said a heavy woman with a badly pock-marked face.

"Carl, and I love Terri's brownies, caramel bars, chocolate chip cookies . . ."

"Okay, we get it," a woman to Cole's right huffed.

"Simone and I love all of you," a thin, African-American woman said, choking back tears.

Several people in the group offered a "we love you, too."

"My name is Eddie. I love—" There was a pause as the Asian man in the dark blue sweatshirt wiggled in his seat. "I love—" He looked down and shook his head. The room grew uncomfortably silent.

Cole glanced from face to face. Several people in the room closed their eyes.

Father John nodded, and a dark-complexioned man, possibly Hispanic, with a beard and sunglasses, leaned forward and said, "I love Eddie." He cleared his throat and said, "Oh yeah, I answer to Enrique."

A murmur of approval came from the group. Eddie didn't look up.

"Lei and I are all about loving people." The bubbly voice came from a very pretty girl in a red T-shirt with "I Love Iris Chang" emblazoned across the chest. "Your turn!" she said, turning to the anorexic woman on her right.

"I'm Kimberley, and I love getting out of the house to come here." There was more than a trace of sarcasm in her voice.

"My name is Mark. I love the freedom this group has given me to be open."

"Hi, I'm Teresa," the woman on Cole's right began. "I love men."

The group chuckled at what appeared to be an inside joke.

Cole sat up a little straighter and said, "As I said before, I'm Cole and I love my granddaughter, Jenny."

"You ain't no grandpa!" Simone blurted out.

"'Fraid so." Cole smiled.

The woman who huffed about Carl's love of baked goods sniffed and said, "I'm Corrine. I love solitude."

Cole looked beyond Corinne and saw a slight androgynous figure, anxiously biting its nails. A pair of flashing blue eyes darted about the group and then up at Father John. "Blank, tonight I'm Blank. I love palaces."

"Last week, she was Clover," Corinne whispered. "I call her 'Nut Case'."

"Thank you. Last week we talked about beginnings. Not just our lives but our rebirths, beginnings of our own choosing. Tonight, I want us to think about those fresh starts. Can they become as big a problem as our old selves?"

"I'm not sure, I'm Blank," Corrine said under her breath.

Father John shot her a disapproving look.

"When'd *you* start over, Father? You haven't always been a priest," Teresa asked coyly.

The question obviously made the priest uncomfortable. "This really isn't about me."

"Weak," Enrique grunted.

"It's only fair. Answer the question," Corinne said, obviously enjoying Father John's discomfort.

"All right. Yes, I did start over. That is how I became a priest."

"You been raped, too?" Eddie said softly.

"No," Father John offered.

"Don't disrespect the Father!" Simone said angrily.

"No, it's okay, Simone. If I am going to lead you from your dark places, I should be willing," the priest paused, "able, to tell you about mine."

"That why priests do little kids?" Enrique said, sitting up in his chair.

"Off topic and way out of line," Mark said, strongly making sure Enrique went no further.

"Look, some of us, as we learn every week, have been hurt deeper or have recovered faster than others. It doesn't mean the hurt isn't just as real or the pain just as great. By God's grace, we are all healing," Father John began. "That is what this group is about, God's grace and victory through his Son. We can't do it alone. We haven't done it alone. That's why we are here. I pray for each of you through the week. Sometimes in my weakness and inability to know what to say, I just pray you will show up to the next group. If your healing requires me to expose my hurt and my need for healing, I am willing."

"Do it," Blank whispered harshly.

"*Can* you do it? I mean is it too painful to open up?" Lei asked.

"We'll see." Father John moved from around the table and placed a chair in front of the group.

Cole wished he had chosen another night to visit the group. This was too personal, too uncomfortable. What was worse, the members of this group understood the dynamic unfolding before them. Cole didn't.

"When I was 18, I met a girl named Maura Kathleen, freshman semester at Holy Cross. I saw her first in English and then discovered she lived on the same floor; she was just down the hall from me. We soon became the best of friends." The priest cleared his throat and continued. "I loved her from the start, but she didn't see me that way. I loved her smile, her unruly curls, and the way she wore a Yankees hat to cover them up. I used to love the way she could go up to one of the professors and talk to him like they were friends. I think all the boys were convinced she could walk on air."

The priest was no longer talking to the group. He was transported, lost in his memories and once again a student at Holy Cross.

"Second semester, Maurie and I—Maurie was her nickname—got an apartment together off campus.

"What a time it was. Every night, we listened to Dylan, the Beatles, Leonard Cohen, and clouds of swirling marijuana smoke filled the air. We would talk endlessly of philosophy, injustice, and politics. We spoke of the things we no longer believed in and how we would change the world."

"You smoke, Father?" Eddie asked in astonishment.

"Not anymore. But that apartment was something else. I loved it. And I loved Maurie. We went everywhere together, did everything together. We would walk that old neighborhood late at night with never a care or a moment of fear. We felt real freedom for the first time in our lives. No more nuns threatening us with hell, no more fierce scoldings from Sister Whoever, and no parents looking over our shoulders." Cole was caught up in the story. Father John's ability to give sermons translated into his personal story well.

Father John continued. "Then things changed. Maurie went out with Gary, a junior she met at a baseball game towards the end of the year. When I met him, it was all I could do to hold back my tears, fears, and anger. I knew she was drifting away from me, and I was afraid to say anything about it. Then she made love with Gary, right under the crucifix above her bed. I only knew because she told me and made me swear I wouldn't tell anyone. My heart was breaking, but she never knew.

"One night at dinner, she just stared at her food. I saw tears; somehow I knew, but I was afraid to ask for fear of the answer. She was late because something began to grow inside her." The man in the chair was no longer a priest but a sad broken boy of 18 looking back and seeing his life through the clarity of time.

"She borrowed some money from me and from some kids at school. She wouldn't tell Gary. She just started school and wasn't about to get married. She learned of an old black woman who helped out college girls 'in trouble.' I told her I loved her and I would marry her. She just said she wished she was dead. I remember how we walked down this long alley looking for the number on the back door of a bar.

"We knocked on the door and a black man with blood-red eyes opened it, took and counted our money. We were taken up a dark flight of stairs, and the old woman appeared from behind a pale green door. I let go of Maurie's hand, and the old woman took her into the room. I sat in a wooden chair in the hallway and waited.

"A few minutes later, the door flew open and Maurie grabbed my hand, and I followed her outside. She couldn't do it. She said there were all these knives and instruments laid out, and she couldn't go through with it. I followed her down the stairs and out onto the street. She was angry and confused, and all the way home we cried. I didn't know what to say to ease her pain." The priest breathed deeply through his nose and soldiered on.

"The next day when I returned from class, I found Maurie. She was laying in what seemed an ocean of blood on the white tile floor of the bathroom. She'd heard that you can do it with a knitting needle." Father John looked down at the floor for a long moment, and Cole thought he wouldn't continue, but again he cleared the lump from his throat and went on, "Once I thought I saw Maurie reading under our favorite tree on the quad, another time at a flea market. Years went by. At our five-year reunion, there was no mention of my Maura Kathleen O'Hare, only stares, and snide whispers.

"It was a long time before I took communion. I blamed God for taking Maurie. He had nothing to do with it. I know that now." Father John seemed to strengthen.

"She made her decision, just like each of us, every day deciding to give in to doubt and self-pity or to rise above it and be victorious. We are no longer victims. I struggled with guilt and grief for nearly 10 years before God showed me his bigger plan." Father John looked from face to face and slapped his palms on the tops of his thighs. "That's when I entered the priesthood. I have to be honest, though, even now when I light a candle I say a prayer and whisper her name."

"I didn't do it to me," Blank said in a harsh growl.

Cole was amazed at the vehemence that the tiny girl projected toward the priest. As he watched the group, he could see that they were readying for battle. The relaxed, slumped posture that accompanied the telling of Father John's story shifted to a ridged, formal position. Every person in the group turned slightly in their chair to face Blank.

"No you didn't," the priest said in a kind but controlled response.

"I killed 'em and I'd do it again. He had no right to do that to me. My body, my soul, my body, my soul." She rocked back and forth, her arms tightly folded across her chest.

"He is dead, it's true. But you didn't kill him. Your father cut his wrists. He did it himself. Your reporting his abuse did not kill him. Just like my Maurie; she didn't have to try to give herself an abortion. She could have lived. The baby could have lived. There are consequences for our actions. What we have to learn is that the actions of others do not have to control our lives. We can and should decide how we live. We must set boundaries for what we let in and what we push out of our lives. I could have spent the rest of my life angry at God and blaming myself for Maurie's death. But *I* didn't kill her, did I? I didn't get her pregnant, either. But I was taking responsibility for things I had no control over." Blank's rocking slowed slightly.

"You could not control what he did to you. He had the power of size and strength and the power of being the adult in a child's world. But look what you had the power to do." The priest paused. "Look at me," he said very softly. "You took the power back. You said 'no more,' and you called the police. From that moment, you were free. He never touched you again, did he?"

"They locked him up."

"Right. They did it. The police, the law, society—all was there to protect you. Your father opened his own veins. Before he was tried, before he even went to court, he chose to die. To run away from what he did. You have to choose, Robin, you have to decide to take control of your life. Your father is dead. It has been 10 years. You are not the little abused child any longer; you are a woman who lives, works and survives in the world on her own. You can't continue to let a dead man cast a shadow over your life."

The young woman was sitting up and no longer rocking. Tears were running down her cheeks. The rest of the people in the group seemed to collectively exhale.

"So, I choose to be free of my cousin Tim!" Lei said brightly.

"I can't take back the scars inside me. I still can't have a child. I still hate the son of a bitch who used me over and over and over. What do I do with that? I won't let him off that easy." Corinne glared at the priest as she spoke.

"I understand why you hate him. If he were here, I would help you beat him. But we don't know where he is, do we? You don't know for sure after all these years if he is even alive. So, how much are you hurting him with your hatred?"

"Yeah, yeah, I'm only hurting myself."

"Well, aren't you?"

"I know how she feels," Eddie spoke for the first time. "I can't take a shit without bleeding. Every day, that blood reminds me of what happened. They messed me up good. Not just in my head. They were supposed to take care of me. Not use me like a whore. How can I forget that?"

"I said nothing about forgetting. We will never forget our hurt, our sorrow, our pain. We all bear scars that will never disappear. What we must do is not let it control us. Otherwise, they are still in control; all those who abused or misused or treated us badly are in control. That is what this is about, control. Eddie, your physical scars, like Corinne's, may never heal." The priest looked down. His shoulders began to shake. He put his hands over his face and began to weep.

"It's all too much," Mark said as he got up and moved toward Father John.

Mark put his hand on the priest's shoulder and stood quietly. One by one, the group stood and made their way over to the priest.

"We are all family, like it or not," Carl said, crossing the room and standing in front of Cole. "We are bound by our past. Our common abuse experience makes us closer than most families. I think we will be stronger after tonight. Some of these newer people don't know how long Corinne and Robin have been coming to this group. They don't understand the dynamics. I have been here the longest. Five years and counting. I've outlasted three priests and a shrink. They have both been here about three years. Robin looks freaky, but she is really a nice person down deep. She never forgets my birthday. Corrine just likes to act tough. This guy," he pointed in Father John's direction, "he's pretty new, too, only been doing the group about a year."

"Tough job," Cole offered.

"Leading or attending?" Carl smiled. "Looks like we're done for tonight, huh?"

"How long does it usually run?" Cole asked.

"Hour or so, depends on who brings treats. No treats tonight, so I'm out of here. Nice to meet you."

"You, too," Cole said, standing.

"You're not leaving, are you?" said a voice coming up behind him.

Cole turned to see Teresa, the one who loved men, approaching with a look that reminded him of a shark on the cover of *National Geographic*.

"Thought I would get going," Cole said, still moving.

"We usually don't bring the priest to tears. You should stick around and meet everybody."

"Maybe next time."

"What's the matter, scared of girls?" Teresa asked, rocking on the side of her foot.

"No, I really came to talk to Father John, but he seems a bit indisposed at the moment."

"I always thought he was gay. It was good to hear the girlfriend story. Means I got a chance."

"He's a priest," Cole said flatly.

"So?"

"Celibacy and all that?"

"Rules are meant to be broken," Teresa said in a fake whisper, giving Cole a wink.

Cole turned and stepped towards her. "So, how long have *you* been coming here?"

"Six months, little more."

"What have you learned so far?"

"The wounded are easiest to finish off." She laughed.

"That's your plan, to finish off the male population?"

"What are you, a shrink?"

"Nope, newspaperman. I came here to get some information on child abuse. I misunderstood; I thought this group was for the parents of abused kids."

"Yeah, you got that part wrong, all right. We are the leftover waste material."

"Tell me, Teresa, what do you do when you're not picking up men at support groups?"

"For a job, you mean?"

"Yeah, how do you fill your days?"

"I work for the post office, letter carrier. Neither sleet nor hail—"

"Do you think there is any hope?"

"For the post office?"

"For anyone who's been molested."

"I wasn't molested. The only ones who talk in here are the ones that got noodled with as a kid. Those of us who got beat on sit quietly and take it all in."

"If it is just about them, why do you bother coming?"

"From time to time, the poor sexual causalities are quiet enough for one of us to get a word in. Your buddy, Carl, he's got a story to tell. Enrique's got scars on him you would never believe."

"And you?"

"Blind in this eye, and I can't smell a thing." Teresa wiggled her nose. "Are you doing a story on the group?"

"Actually, I'm working on the murders of three little girls. The last victim, Lucy Zhang, was a member of this parish. Her parents spoke highly of Father John, and that's why I came tonight."

"The ultimate abuse. I always figured my old man would beat me to death, but I survived. But murder isn't abuse. No scars on the dead, nothing to outlive or outrun. If I have learned one thing coming here, it is that we all have emotional scars as well as physical ones, but we all wear them differently. I've been to psychiatrists and therapists for years, and I understand that I throw myself at men to make me feel in control. I understand it, but I don't change it. It feels good. After all those years of being knocked around, anyone who holds me close and gives or takes pleasure from my body is okay with me. So long as I'm not used as a punching bag, I love being touched. My fear is that when the face wrinkles up and the tits go south, I won't know where to turn. So, what do you do with somebody like me? It's like smoking, you know, it's not healthy but you do it anyway."

Cole smiled at the frank understanding Teresa showed. "Well," he said, "mind if I use some of *that* for my article?"

"Me? Quoted? Fantastic." Teresa smiled. "You know, I've never been with a newspaperman." She gave Cole a smile that showed her ironic wit more than her need for conquest.

"I'll keep that in mind," Cole said, offering his hand. "Good to meet you."

"You really should give the group another shot. Tonight was kind of a weird one. It's been building and they finally found the priest's weak spot. That's the thing you learn around here, that the abused are really good at abuse. Find a weakness and attack it. It's the rage inside; give it a chance, and it flares up and burns whatever is nearby." For a brief moment, Teresa let her guard down, and Cole saw a fragile, tender expression cross her face. This glimpse at the real Teresa made him realize she was well on her way to recovery.

Cole smiled and made his way to the door.

The next morning, Cole was surprised to find a call waiting for him when he got to the *Chronicle*.

"Cole Sage."

"You are a hard man to track down, Viejo."

Cole smiled at the hoarse sound of Anthony Perez on the phone. The journalism student that Cole was so fond of was winding down his first year of college. The transformation from "Whisper", the street thug, to the dean's list, was the stuff of *Reader Digest* stories, but something Cole would never write about. They found each other at a time when both were ready for and needed a change. Somehow, the two men from such different worlds recognized in the other their common desire to learn constantly. Cole made it possible for Anthony to go to college, and he flourished.

"I've been meaning to call you, but I have got caught up in a whirlwind. I got a job out here at the *Chronicle*. Erin and Ben have moved to San Francisco, too. I wrote to you about that right?"

"I can't believe you're leaving the *Sentinel*. What did Mr. Brennan say?"

"That's the downside to the whole thing. He hasn't much longer, and he wanted me gone before he—" Cole paused. "He thought it would be good for me to take a new job before the new editor came in. Things get shaken up with a changing of the guard. But, hey, you called me! What's going on?" Cole was happy to change the subject.

"I have a chance for a summer internship at the *Tribune*. Nothing for certain, but I look pretty solid on paper. My advisor said a letter of reference from somebody outside of school could help a lot. So, who better than an old newshound, eh?"

The "eh" sounded foreign and odd coming from Anthony. Cole wondered if it was an intentional affectation or if he just slipped back into his old speech pattern. He went through such a change in the last year that no one would ever dream he once headed a street gang deeply involved in criminal enterprise. Except for the soft hoarseness that earned him the nickname 'Whisper', he was a different man.

"E-mail me the details, and I'll get it right out. Hey, if it doesn't work out, maybe I can get you one out here."

"That would be nice, but you know, I think the more time I am out of California probably the better it will be."

After a bit more catching up, they rang off.

Cole stared down at the notes, outlines, and ideas jotted down on scraps of receipts, napkins, and lunch bags in front of him that were becoming the framework of the story he would write. Throughout his career, he wrote of murder, rape, mayhem, war, and every form of unspeakable cruelty that human beings can do to each other, yet this story was different. The murders of the three little girls and one traumatized survivor were somehow more personal.

At dinner the night before, with Jenny on his knee, *Grandfather* Cole Sage could not get the parents of Lucy Zhang out of his thoughts. Their precious child snatched from their family without warning and left broken like so many dried twigs. Their loss became Cole's pain, too.

When Jenny went to bed, Ben explained to Erin the connection between the girls, leaving out the gruesome details. Cole related the hopeless feeling within the police force at having no leads and no clues. What was once an unthinkable crime seemed almost routine in a nation of senseless serial murders. Try as they may, the police were victims, too, and being held at bay by a killer who made only one mistake. Had he panicked? Was he seen?

For whatever reason, the killer left the most damning evidence of all, a witness who looked him in the face. The only chance of catching him was Camilla, a child so traumatized by her would-be killer's sexual assault, and the beating and abandonment of her father, all she could do was babble.

There was a sense of relief that the authorities finally admitted a connection between the other girls and the death of Lucy Zhang. Still, shutting it all off came hard, and as Cole finally drifted to sleep that night, he held a prayer on his lips for the safety of his beautiful granddaughter sleeping in the next room.

FOURTEEN

The sign above the door read "Research Monsters, Inc." Randy Callen and the other cyber-ninjas in the bowels of the *Chronicle* took great pride in their "independently weird" status. They spoke on the phone a couple of times, and Randy wrote Cole a very nice thank-you letter when he got the job, but this would be their first face-to-face meeting since they first met a little over a year ago.

"Mr. Sage! What's goin' on?" Randy said, jumping to his feet and offering Cole his misshapen hand in welcome.

Cole grasped Randy's wrist, engulfing the frail twisted form of the young man's right hand in his large grip. "Fancy meeting you here." Cole smiled.

"Never figured on this, Mr. Sage." The young man's face beamed with his pride at being on the same team as the man whose name alone got him his job.

"Please call me Cole." He gave Randy a pat on the shoulder and asked, "Still able to snoop around?" With a jerk of his head, Cole indicated the room full of research wunderkinders.

Randy lowered his voice and whispered, "These guys are nuts. They do things I would never have dreamed of, at least, not until I got here. What do you need?"

"Data on child abductions, child murders, and serial pedophiles. I want to get a picture of the guy who is killing these little girls. A profile. There has got to be something the police aren't telling us, you know? Maybe the feds have something."

"Now you're talking." Randy grinned like a kid about to toilet paper the principal's house. "Mind if I enlist some help?"

"Your call. This isn't just for a story, Randy. This guy has to be stopped."

"Yes, sir. I'll get right on it," Randy said, nodding seriously.

"When I get out here permanently, we need to have lunch. I owe you."

"You don't owe me anything, Mr. Sage—Cole; I could never have gotten this job without you."

"Then lunch ought to just about even the score." Cole smiled. "Call me when you get something." Cole bent and wrote his cell phone number on a Post-It note.

On his way to the elevator, Cole remembered he needed to finish his paperwork in the personnel office. As he went through the door, he heard Beth Swann's throaty laugh. As expected, three of her admirers were gathered around her cubicle.

"Mr. Sage!" she called out, spotting Cole. "Nice to see you again." And as if on cue, the fan club disbanded.

"Hello. I just remembered I have some paperwork to finish."

Beth stood and crossed the aisle and spoke into a cubicle. "Phillip, this is Cole Sage. He's joining the paper and needs to set up or transfer or whatever you do to retirement stuff. Can you help him?"

"I suppose so," a less-than-enthusiastic voice sighed from the cubicle.

Beth looked at Cole and, as she cleared sight of the cubicle, put her index finger in her mouth and did an exaggerated fake-gagging face.

Cole stuck his head into the cubicle and said, "Hi. I'm Cole Sage."

"Yeah, that's what she said. Have a seat." The man in the cubicle did not look up.

"So, how do we transfer my account from Chicago out to here?"

"Is it a 401k, Keogh, ERISA, Roth, IRA, what? Are you vested?" Phillip Wesley Ashcroft snapped.

Cole stood up and stuck his head outside the cubicle.

"What are you doing?"

"I was looking for the AARP sign."

"The what?"

"*American Association of Retired Persons*, I figured I missed the turn and wound up there."

"Hilarious. Can we continue?"

"What was your name again?" Cole said with a forced smile.

"Ashcroft. Phillip Ashcroft." He did not give his special name.

"You like your job, Phil?" Cole sensed anger and hostility that seemed to seep from the pores of the pale man in front of him.

"Not particularly. It's Phillip," Phillip Wesley Ashcroft said with a condescending groan.

"That was my guess," Cole began. "I used to hate my job, my life, actually. Then, you know, the strangest thing happened, Phil. I realized that *I* was the one out of step. Everybody else was having a great time, and I was the fly in the oatmeal. You, my friend, need a change of scenery."

"Are you finished?"

"Has it done any good?" Cole frowned.

"Hardly," Phillip Wesley Ashcroft sneered.

"That's a shame. Look, Phil, I haven't a clue what kind of plan I have because I have been alone most of my adult life. Until recently, I really didn't care how long I lived or what happened."

"Are you going to start telling me about Jesus?" Phillip Wesley Ashcroft interlaced his fingers and placed them on the desk in front of him.

"No, unless you think that would help. I could tell you about Jenny."

"And who is that?" Phillip Wesley Ashcroft sneered and cocked his head to one side as if to say, "I'll wait until you finish."

"My granddaughter."

"How sweet." Ashcroft gave Cole an unnatural smile.

"I just think that it's more fun to be happy than a sourpuss and you, Phil, are a sourpuss. Now, take those fellas that hang around Beth's cubicle."

"Idiots!"

"Exactly the point I was about to make. She wouldn't give them the time of day. But just living in hope that she *might,* makes them happy and gives them a reason to come to work."

"She's a bitch."

"Harsh. Did you ask her out, Phil?"

"*Phillip*, and I don't think that is any of your concern."

"See, you got to roll with it. I bet Beth has rejected those idiots a dozen times, but it doesn't keep them from enjoying the chase. Lighten up, Phil, life's too short."

"Is that the secret, Mr. Sage, embrace your rejection?" Phillip Wesley Ashcroft's tone was cold and pure hatred.

"I don't know, but you attract more flies with honey than vinegar, right?" And with that, Cole stood up and stepped across the aisle. "Beth. How about lunch today?"

"Sure, that would be fun!" Beth put both hands over her mouth to squelch a laugh. It was obvious she was listening and enjoying Cole's attempt to reform Phillip Ashcroft.

Cole went back and sat down across from Phillip Wesley Ashcroft and smiled. "See, a little friendliness gets the job done every time."

"I find your condescending manner and flippant interference in my affairs offensive and insulting, Mr. Sage. In the future, please confine any conversation we may have to the status of your retirement package as provided by this company. Am I clear?" Phillip Wesley Ashcroft's face was ablaze with repressed rage.

"I am truly sorry if I offended you, Mr. Ashcroft. I have been where you are, and it is no fun. My only thought was to help you realize there is a way out. I won't bother you again. I'll e-mail you the information on my Chicago account when I receive it." Cole stood and moved to the aisle between the cubicles. "You know, Mr. Ashcroft, anger is a time bomb, it can ruin your life. Try to find something to make you happy before it's too late." As Cole passed Beth's cubicle, he softly said, "Meet you in the lobby at 12?" She nodded.

Phillip Wesley Ashcroft did not respond. Reaching into his desk drawer for a white plastic bottle, he squirted a glob of his homemade hand lotion into his palm. He rubbed the tops of his hands repeatedly and massaged the lotion into his skin. "I have something that makes me happy," he muttered. "I bring salvation. I save the world from future cruel bitches like Beth." He fairly vomited out the last few words.

He would find another girl to save. He would do it today. He must leave soon. He would have to wait, though, until Beth returned from lunch with her newfound *boyfriend*. The desire was so strong, Phillip

Wesley Ashcroft could barely remain seated. He closed his eyes and pictured a sweet little girl with a box of Cracker Jacks. She offered him the prize. His rage began to recede. He would go find her at lunch. He imagined walking hand in hand with her through Golden Gate Park. Moment by moment, his anger eased, and he was a child again.

Cole was late getting downstairs to the lobby, but Beth Swann patiently waited by the front door. She gave him a brilliant smile as he waved hello.

"So, where to?" Cole asked.

"There's a new little Japanese place around the corner, want to give it a try?"

"Sounds great."

The small talk they made as they walked to the restaurant centered on the weather. Most of the way, they walked in silence, bobbing and weaving through the noontime crush of people on the street. The Katsu was small, but already attracting a good lunch crowd. Cole spoke to the hostess in his limited, but charmingly effective, Japanese and she took them to a table in the corner near a window.

"*And* he speaks Japanese. The wonders of the Wondrous Mr. Sage never end." Beth teased but was impressed. "Sorry about Phillip's flare-up."

"Hey, I was out of line. Not your fault. Sometimes I don't know when to shut up. Must be support group hangover."

"Support group?"

"Yeah, I went to a sexual abuse support group last night to talk to a priest and must have still felt the urge to reach out." Cole offered an embarrassed raise of his eyebrows. "The parents of Lucy Zhang, the last little girl murdered, spoke very highly of their priest, and I thought he might have some insights or thoughts to add background to the story I'm working on."

"Maybe Phillip should go to a support group of some kind. That guy is really creepy. Did you see his hands? They look just like a woman's."

Cole sat up straight in his chair. "What did you say?" he urged.

"I said he gives me the creeps."

"No, no, about his hands," Cole insisted.

"Didn't you notice? They are as smooth as silk and not a hair on them. They look just like a woman's in a hand lotion ad."

"Oh, God," Cole gasped. He could feel his heart racing and his face go flush as he fumbled for the cell phone in his pocket. He hit the number for Ben's phone. "Pick up, come on!"

Beth sat across the table and stared at Cole like he suddenly had lost his mind.

"Ben? Cole. What did you say that the little girl, Camilla....what did she say about her attacker's hands?"

"Como las manos de una mujer, it means 'like a woman's hands.' Why?"

"I've found the killer."

Within 10 minutes, Lt. Leonard Chin arrived at the Katsu restaurant. Outside, four patrol cars idled, their occupants awaiting instructions. Cole described

Ashcroft and made a case for how closely he fit the profile of the man they were looking for. But hands were the link. "Like a woman's hands" is what Camilla kept saying. Beth described how Ashcroft frequently used lotion and how smooth and hairless his hands were.

"The little girl is our only witness. I really don't know if she can make an ID without going into a tailspin. Ben says she isn't much better than when they brought her in." The detective rotated his cell phone in his hand as he spoke.

"Ashcroft doesn't know that," Cole interjected.

"There is that. You want to come along? It's a hell of an angle for your story." Chin smiled.

"How about me?" Beth broke in for the first time.

"You *do* have to go back to your desk." Cole smiled. "This kid's got the heart of a reporter. Should we let her tag along?"

Cole and Leonard Chin waited behind the grey double doors separating the personnel department and the short hallway leading to the elevators and watched as Beth made her way to her desk.

"How was your date?" called out a voice from behind a cubicle.

"Very interesting, Tim." Beth shot back, trying to sound flirtatious.

"If you're looking for interesting—" a second voice began.

"Mr. Sage is a whole other level, Eric." The banter with her admirers helped to calm Beth as she approached her desk. "I'm ba-a-ack." Beth half sang toward Phillip Wesley Ashcroft's cubicle.

Without a word, Ashcroft stood and made his way to the back of the office. His thoughts raced with anticipation as he imagined the smile of a pale blonde girl approaching him across a grassy, shaded park.

Beth held her breath and didn't look up as he passed her desk.

There was a long frozen moment as Phillip Wesley Ashcroft came through the door into the hallway. Cole stood to the right of the doors against the wall next to the elevator. A flash of anger, then apprehension, crossed Ashcroft's face as their eyes met. Before either could speak, Leonard Chin approached Ashcroft from the left.

"Phillip Ashcroft, you have the right to remain silent. Anything you say can and will—"

"Mr. Sage, is this when I am supposed to embrace my rejection, or is this a new form of acceptance?" Ashcroft spoke without guile or emotion.

"—be used against you in a court of law," Chin continued, unfazed by Ashcroft's interruption. "You have the right to have an attorney present during questioning. If you cannot afford an attorney, one will be appointed for you. Do you understand these rights?"

"I wish to be addressed and referred to as Phillip Wesley Ashcroft at all times."

"Do you understand these rights?" Chin pressed.

"What is it you think I have done?"

"I have read you your rights, Mr. Ashcroft, as required by federal law. Do you understand them?" Chin's tone hardened.

"Of course. What is this about?" Ashcroft said, void of emotion.

"You are under arrest for the murder of Lucy Zhang and the attempted murder of Camilla Salguero."

"That's all?" Ashcroft smiled, turning to face Leonard Chin for the first time.

Chin spread his feet ever so slightly. "No, I will do everything in my power to tie you to the deaths of two other girls as well."

The elevator doors opened, and Ashcroft glanced at the two women who exited and headed for the offices farther down the hall.

"Do you have some form of identification?" Ashcroft snapped.

"How's this?" Chin took Ashcroft's wrist and in an instant, his hands were cuffed behind his back. He removed a radio from his belt and keyed the microphone. "Ready for transport."

"On our way, Lieutenant."

"So, will I make the papers, Mr. Sage?" Ashcroft smiled for the first time since Cole met him.

"Yes, but not for what you've done. The story will be that you have been stopped and what you won't do again."

"What I did, Mr. Sage, was to save those little angels from becoming arrogant, snotty bitches like your new friend, Miss Swann. They are forever frozen in time as sweet, kind, thoughtful, and full of hope, the light of new discoveries sparkling in their eyes."

"There *is* no light, Phillip. You saw to that."

The elevator doors opened and two uniformed officers crossed to where Ashcroft stood. The older of the two nodded to Chin, took Ashcroft by the arm, and guided him to the elevator.

Ashcroft turned and looked at Cole. "You know, Mr. Sage, you have done me a great service. Wherever I go, I now can dwell in the glow of the sweet moments I spent with each of those girls without the restraints and tedium of being forced to work here. I can be alone with my memories and delight in the fantasies I will build around them. Thank you, Mr. Sage."

The elevator doors glided closed.

***

The call came at 1:53 a.m. It took a long moment for Cole to register what the caller was saying. When he did, a wave of numbness came over him.

"Mr. Sage? I'm sorry to inform you that Michael Brennan has passed away."

No one called Brennan 'Michael', Cole thought, *he was Mick to everyone.*

The caller was a charge nurse at Weiss Memorial's Emergency Room. Kind, but efficient and to the point, she continued. "An ambulance brought Mr. Brennan in about 11:30. He was in a coma when they arrived and died peacefully about an hour ago without regaining consciousness. You are listed as next of kin. I am very sorry for your loss."

After asking Cole if he would be making the funeral arrangements, she hung up.

Mick Brennan left specific instructions for his funeral: There wasn't to be one. Friends and colleagues could gather as he was "planted," as he put it, and he asked that Cole say a few words before they "threw dirt in his face." As Cole reviewed the clearly labeled documents Mick left in a file folder on the kitchen table in his apartment, he wasn't sure if this was an attempt at humor or a slap in the face to those who might show up.

With the help of Olajean, Cole wrote an announcement for the graveside service and then distributed it to the few people Mick would have wanted there. As promised, Cole took Mick's obituary to the publisher's office along with a note from Mick requesting it be printed as is. To Cole's great relief, the publisher wasn't in.

With a few words of common condolence and a hug for Mick's secretary, Cole entered his old friend's office and closed the door. Even though he would never enter the room again, Mick Brennan still was very much present. The smell of the cigarettes lingered, and the sweet aroma of his Old Spice aftershave hung in the room like incense.

Cole methodically went about shredding the papers in Mick's desk drawers. The few mementos that Brennan hadn't already taken home were carefully packed in a box that Cole brought up from his office.

An office is a strange thing, Cole thought. All the years a man spends behind a desk in it, all the decisions, all the memos, plans, and orders; all would be forgotten with a new paint job, and someone else's personal effects on the shelves. Mick Brennan was gone. A new editor sat down the hall, prepared to fill this space.

***

The graveside service was scheduled for 11 o'clock. Per Brennan's instructions, there were no pallbearers, and the flowers were limited to one bunch of white chrysanthemums on the casket. The casket of dark mahogany looked handsome with its handles of dull pewter. The mortuary prepared four rows of six chairs. It proved to be about three rows too many.

At 10 minutes after 11, Cole stood and faced the odd mix of colleagues from work, old friends, and a young man in a dark blue suit, white shirt but no tie.

"Michael Francis Brennan was my friend," Cole began. "He was not easy to love. Many of you know that well." Several of the mourners chuckled. "Say what you will, though, I never in all the years I knew him, ever saw Mick hurt anyone intentionally. He was gruff, short-tempered and demanding, but it was all to ensure that the paper he loved was as good as it could possibly be.

"I first met Mick when I did an internship at the *Sentinel*; I was in my early 20s, fresh out of college and ready to take on the world. The first piece I gave him he wadded up and threw in the trash. 'Where the hell did you learn to write?' was all he said as he crumpled it. 'Do it again.' I did, again and then again. I called him every name I could think of while I worked, but over the next six months, he taught me more than I learned in four years of college. He was a hard taskmaster, but it was because he wanted me to be the best newspaperman I could be. When I returned from a stint in Southeast Asia, he gave me my first job at a stateside newspaper. I owe everything I have become as a journalist to him."

Cole cleared his throat and stared down at the casket in front of him. "Mick did not believe in God. So, I can't say he's in a better place or we will see him again. None of the typical things you would say at a funeral seem to apply. He often made fun of my faith, as simple as it is. He would tease me about fairy stories and 'rip-offs' of other religions that he claimed filled the Bible. 'Jesus is cool, but he don't pay the rent' was a favorite of his for poking fun. I'm no saint and would never preach to anyone. But I would be remiss to if I didn't get the last word in our years of theological debate." Cole smiled and looked down at the casket. "So, here you are, Mick, all dressed up and no place to go." Nervous laughter from the mourners broke the silence.

"I doubt a day will go by that I won't think of his rumpled suits and cigarette-burned neckties, and I will never look down at a finished piece of writing without flinching at the thought of the red editing marks he was so famous for bloodying all over what I thought was a finished draft.

"Thank you all for honoring my friend today. I loved Mick Brennan and will miss him dearly. Rest in peace, old friend."

The small group shifted in their seats. Several people wiped their eyes. Silently, one by one, they stood and walked past the casket. Words were softly muttered, and people whispered to each other. The young man in the dark suit remained seated.

The last few to leave shook hands or patted Cole on the shoulder and complimented him on his remarks. Cole turned, closed his eyes, and said a short prayer, asking the Almighty to look past Mick's shortcomings and consider his heart—maybe let him slip in under the gate.

As he turned to leave, he noticed the young man in the dark suit. Still seated in the back row, he had one arm slung across the top of the chair next to him. As Cole passed, the young man stood up.

"I'm Marcus Brennan."

"I figured," Cole said, offering his hand.

"Nice words, pretty much funeral bullshit, but nice words. Everybody's a saint when they die." Marcus waited for a reaction from Cole.

"I said what I felt. Your dad meant a lot to me."

"I tried to get my mom to come. She says he died a long time ago as far as she's concerned. Let the dead bury the dead and good riddance."

"That's too bad. Bitterness can eat you up."

"We got a lot to be bitter about. Your friend was never there for me while I was growing up. That precious newspaper you spoke so fondly of was his family, not us. He never gave a damn about me or my mom."

"I'm sorry. I wish it was different." Cole hoped Marcus felt the sincerity in his words.

"You're the lucky one. It sounds like you got the attention that should have been ours."

"Not really. I don't think in all the years I knew him we ever saw each other outside the *Sentinel* building. Maybe once. Don't read what I said up there wrong. He was an asshole pretty much most of the time. He hurt me deeply many times and angered me most of the rest. I'm sure, though, that down deep, in his own way, he loved me.

"I know he loved you because, until the day he died, your picture was on his desk. Of the few things in his apartment, there was a soccer trophy of yours and three pictures of you. So, don't think of him too harshly in the end. He was what he was, and it wasn't what either of us would have chosen."

"I guess you're right. Doesn't matter much now, does it?" Marcus looked down at his shoes.

"Not much does once they lower you into the ground. If you can, find a good memory to hang onto, and let the rest go." Cole looked over his shoulder at the casket.

Marcus Brennan turned without a word and walked away. Cole thought of mentioning Mick's will. Marcus didn't come for his birthright. Cole wasn't even sure he came to say goodbye. The father and son parted as they lived, wanting the other's approval and never getting it.

FIFTEEN

The morning after the funeral, Cole went to the *Sentinel*. His mind was awash with memories as he pushed open the heavy art deco door that stood between the Chicago wind and the last of the city's original newspapers. Cole was twenty-two the first time he put his hand on the shiny chrome door and he remembered how he felt entering the holy shrine of journalism.

Twenty-five years, a million miles, and uncountable words later, he said his goodbye. He would finish the article on child abduction and murder. The *San Francisco Chronicle* and the *Chicago Sentinel* would jointly publish it. The death of Mick Brennan closed the final chapter on his life in Chicago. Cole dreaded parting with his close friends, but the hard part was over.

Olajean called in sick, so Cole slipped past the fill-in receptionist without a word. He called and asked the janitor for a couple of boxes. When he arrived, a stack of six stood outside his cubicle.

As much as he hated the grey carpeted box that he called home for all the "dark years," there was a sense of comfort in knowing its boundaries. He stared at every square inch of the six-by-eight box at one time or another. There was no muse in this cell, and the first step in the rebirth of Cole Sage was the realization that his only chance of regaining his muse lay outside its carpeted confines.

Two pink call slips lay in his basket, both from Lt. Leonard Chin in San Francisco. Cole tried the number twice but got a voicemail both times. He left a message the second time. "Cole Sage here; got your message. I'll be at this *Sentinel* number for a couple more hours and then I'll be at home."

The few mementos and pictures decorating the desktop and walls packed quickly. Sorting the files, scraps of ideas, articles, and clippings took a lot longer. As he read a piece he clipped from the NY Times, Cole sensed a presence behind him. Turning, he saw his old friend Tom Harris. The detective looked troubled, his tie was uncharacteristically undone.

"Come to help me pack?" Cole said, glancing around at the mess he created.

"We got a problem." Harris's voice and expression were something new to Cole.

"What's going on?" Cole asked.

Harris held up a plain manila envelope. "Is there someplace more private we can talk?"

Cole directed Harris to a small conference room. Harris closed the door behind them and closed the blinds on the small window facing the outer office area.

"This came in the mail today. Thankfully, it was handed over to me. The community service officer that sorts the mail knows we're friends." Harris unclipped the metal clasp and slid the contents of the envelope onto the table.

"What is it?" Cole was becoming uneasy with his friend's cold, emotionless tone.

On the table lay a white 9-by-11 envelope in a plastic evidence bag. Cole's name and Chicago home address were written in black felt-tip pen. There was no return address, and the bottom left-hand edge was partially ripped open, exposing part of a photograph. The picture seemed to be bare flesh. The envelope was ripped open like it was done in a big hurry.

"Where did this come from?" Cole asked, reaching for the bag.

"Somebody dropped it through the mail slot at the precinct. This was on it." Harris slipped his hand in his jacket pocket and handed Cole a yellow Post-It note.

"'Something should be done about perverts like him!'" Cole read aloud. "What is this about, Tom?"

"Take a look."

Harris opened the evidence bag. He pulled out a second smaller plastic bag that held a small stack of 8-by-10 color photographs and a sheet of white paper with a short note.

"There are six photographs, all of children, all engaged in sexual acts with adult males, all more perverse and obscene than the last," Harris said in disgust. He turned the one exposed photo toward Cole.

Repulsed by what he saw, Cole turned it face down. When he looked up at Tom Harris, he was looking into the eyes of a stranger. "I don't understand," Cole said flatly.

"That makes two of us. What have you got to say for yourself?"

"What the hell is that supposed to mean? These aren't mine." Cole stood, his anger flaring.

"Sit down, shut up, and read the note."

The note was a simple printed message on plain white bond paper. "Hope you like these samples. This is the stuff I told you about. The new DVD runs for nearly two hours and is loaded with our kind of action. These little sweethearts really deliver. PayPal payment preferred (you know the account name), and a smoking hot copy will be on its way!" It was not signed, but *Red Hot Angels* was printed in red at the end of the text.

"Well?" Harris finally said.

"Well, what?"

"Look, I'm your friend. If this had gone to somebody else, you'd be in cuffs."

"You think *I* sent for this?" Cole jumped to his feet. His voice was a fierce combination of defiance cut with betrayal.

"I didn't say that. I just want an explanation." Harris' tone softened slightly.

"I haven't got one," Cole shouted. "It's obviously a set-up."

"You got to help me out here. This is really serious. This links you to child pornography! This guy gets busted, and you're on his mailing list."

"When did you get this? You come in here, drop this on me, and expect an explanation? I haven't a clue what this is about." Cole sat back down.

"It came while you were in California." Harris ran his hand through his hair. "Look, the best I can figure is that it arrived ripped at your mailbox. You got an outside mailbox, right? With the little hook thing for magazines and big envelopes? Some snoop in your building saw the pictures sticking out and opened it. The subject matter wasn't what they were hoping for, grossed them out, and they turned it in to us."

"Who would do that?"

"How many people in your building?"

"Okay. I get it. So, what am I supposed to do?"

"We can't just ignore this. Somebody either has a really sick sense of humor, or you are on their shit list big time. You better put on your thinking cap."

Cole spun the envelope on the table repeatedly. He looked at the jagged tear at the opening. As he flipped the envelope over, the clasp was still covered by the flap. It was sealed. He flipped it over again. His gaze fell on the stamps. The stamp on the left was nearly intact, only the bottom corner was torn away. Half of the stamp on the right was gone, torn away diagonally. Neither stamp bore a cancellation mark on them. The envelope was never mailed.

"Look at this. These stamps aren't used," Cole slid the envelope across the table to Harris.

Harris looked at the well-worn envelope. "You're right. I'm going to have a friend of mine in the lab run all this stuff. I should have seen that. You're right. Guess I was just too pissed to see straight."

"Well, Sherlock, that's why you got me." Cole gave a halfhearted laugh.

"If you don't figure this out, you're going to always wonder if some freak out there's got your name on his list." Harris slapped Cole's shoulder with the envelope as he made his way to the door.

Harris stopped and turned, "By the way, I never thought it was yours for a second."

"Gee, thanks. You had me fooled," Cole said sarcastically.

"As far as I'm concerned, this never happened. But it's kind of like pricking your finger on a needle in a junkie's pocket. You always wonder if you're gonna have HIV show up on your next blood test."

"Thanks for having my back, Tom."

Harris smiled, nodded, and closed the door.

The initial panic subsided, and Cole was left with seething anger. He stared at the table top. He ran through the names and faces of some of the lowlifes he had run-ins with over the years, but this wasn't their kind of payback. A letter bomb maybe, a death threat and some white powder to put everyone in a panic, maybe even a dead rat in a box, but this was too real. The higher-class enemies he made were more likely to sue in an effort to cost him time and money that they knew he couldn't afford to lose.

As he walked back to his cubicle Cole's mind raced trying to think of who would pull such a vile stunt. His thoughts were interrupted by the ringing phone at his desk.

"Sage," Cole said, answering the phone.

"Cole, its Leonard Chin," the voice on the other end offered.

"Hello. How's it going?"

"We're building quite a case against your buddy Ashcroft."

"My buddy?"

"Every time I interview him, he asks if he can write or call you to thank you for helping him break his shackles. It's not everybody who has somebody so grateful." Chin laughed. "Hey, I think I might have something you can help with."

"Sure, whatever you need."

"How far are you from Plainfield?"

"About 40 minutes, depending on traffic. Why?"

"We've been going through Ashcroft's apartment with a fine-tooth comb. Turned up something of interest. Thing is, I need to kind of keep it off the radar. Have you got anybody in the Chicago PD that can do some sniffing around and keep quiet about it? I mean *really* quiet?"

"A good friend of mine. He just left here a few minutes ago."

"I'm famous for my bad timing. Here's the deal. We found a couple of kiddy porn DVDs postmarked *Plainfield, Illinois*. Outfit calls itself *Red Hot Angels*."

"It's Terry," Cole said, almost in a whisper.

"What?"

"We won't need a cop. Can I call you back?"

"Of course, no big hurry. Let me know what you find out—but, Cole, it is really important this doesn't leak."

"Don't worry, I won't tell a soul." Cole hung up.

Cole reached into the box and pulled out the envelope and note. *Red Hot Angels*. He ran his fingers over the stamps on the envelope.

***

Terry Kosciuszko's anger and self-hatred were like a snake eating its tail. He hated his weight, yet he fed his unmet desires with massive amounts of sweets, which only made him gain more. More than once, he had stomped on a half-eaten box of doughnuts and kicked them across the kitchen floor. He broke every mirror in the house. Just a glimpse of his massive girth would set him off in an uncontrollable spiral of destructive rage.

The arousal he once got from his collection of pictures, tapes, DVDs, and his hours in Internet chat rooms waned. More and more, he found himself thinking of going out and finding a child. He burned for the touch of soft skin and the feel and movement of another human being. All that stopped him was fear. Fear of getting caught, fear of it not being enough, and fear of rejection. Taking what you dreamed of was a far cry from what you dreamed of being freely offered. So he searched to find new and even more deviant ways to feed the demons within.

When it didn't work, his anger turned to Jeff and Sophie —his perfect brother, his perfect wife, and their perfect little family. They were all that stood in his way. It was his ranch, his house, and his to sell. They were all that was keeping him from fulfilling his dream to move to Thailand or the Philippines or some other place where they turn a blind eye to lovers of the young. If he could sell this stupid piece of dirt, he would be gone. He could live out his days happily and with the love he so longed for. He would be a god, worshipped for what he could provide a child bride, or maybe two, possibly even three. He would be the master of a harem of child brides. All that stopped him was Jeff's unwillingness to give him what was his.

Terry's old green truck shook and rattled as he made his way to his brother's house. He had no plan, but he would know what to do when he got there. They were such cowards. He scared them before. He would ramp up his game. If his brother wasn't convinced by Terry's willingness to kill and maim their pets, maybe he needed to take a bolder step.

The truck rolled to a stop across the street from the long driveway. His message on the white fence was painted over. The blossoms and greens of spring made his brother's house look like a cover of *Better Homes and Gardens*. Terry removed every bit of foliage from the farm. His first thought was that he didn't want to be bothered. The truth was he hated the sight of living things. He soaked the ground with powerful herbicides. He set traps and laid out poison everywhere to kill any rodent or varmint that might wander on to his near-lunar landscape. He sprayed for insects and was relatively sure the property was devoid of any flora and fauna.

Just to the left of the garage, Terry's eye caught a flash of movement. A large bush shook, and a moment later, Sophie came around to the front of the large shrub with a pair of hedge trimmers in her hand. His pulse quickened. *She was outside,* he thought. His mind raced. What could he do? He left the truck and started making his way up the long driveway. He stayed close to the fence so as not to draw attention to himself. Sophie snipped, whacked, and trimmed the bush, stepping back to survey her work. Terry moved closer.

For a few moments, he lost sight of Sophie. Their Chevy Tahoe was parked in the driveway, blocking his view. It also blocked Sophie's view should she turn around. Terry's breathing was hard and shallow. He was not used to walking more than the few feet from the house to the truck or to the ATV he used to ride around the farm. When he reached the car, he bent over with his hands on his knees trying to catch his breath and think of what to do next. His time was cut short; Sophie moved toward the house. He couldn't let her go inside! He began to panic.

He moved quickly and got in front of her. Put her between him and the Tahoe. "Nice day," Terry panted.

"What are you doing here?" Sophie stood straight, and her tone was cold and demanding.

"'While back, a friend of yours paid me a little visit. I thought it was only right to return the courtesy. He's not very nice, your friend. He said some very unpleasant things to me." Terry's words came in short breathless bursts. He was sweating heavily and his face flushed bright red.

"We thought if Cole talked to you, you might drop all this foolishness about Jeff signing over his share of the farm to you." Sophie tried to move to get a better shot at running for the house, but Terry shifted and moved closer with her every movement.

"I really don't like you talking to strangers about my business. I've tried really hard to send you subtle messages. My brother is stealing what my mother meant for me. It's mine, and it is my ticket out of here." He moved within a few short feet of Sophie. Her back nearly touched the side of the car.

"We have a restraining order. You need to leave." For the first time, fear showed in her voice. She raised the hedge clipper.

Terry's hand flew out and knocked the clipper from her hand. "You see, that's what I mean. We're family. You shouldn't do things like that." Terry suddenly shot forward and pushed Sophie back against the wheel well. Her lower back hit hard against the trim over the tire.

"Let me go!" Sophie demanded.

Terry threw his thick arm across Sophie's collarbone and pressed her against the vehicle. She was bent back across the car, making it difficult to breathe.

Terry pressed close to her body and began rubbing against her.

"Isn't this more friendly?" he huffed. His hot breath was foul in her face.

"Get off me." Sophie's words were choked. Terry's arm moved up and was heavy across her throat.

"We're just getting—" Terry gave a sharp thrust of his hips, "—comfy."

Sophie felt his thick hand fumbling with her T-shirt. He slid his rough hand under her shirt and stroked her stomach. "Now, isn't that nice?" he said softly. She felt the tips of his fingers hit the bottom of her bra.

"Let me—" Sophie's words were cut short as Terry's arm pressed hard against her neck.

In a quick push of his hand, Sophie's bra was pushed up over her breast and she felt his thick rough hands move across her nipple. "There is... More here... Than I... Ever dreamed." Terry's words were accentuated with a sharp hard squeezing of her breast.

Sophie realized she was completely powerless. Twice she started to black out and saw bursts of stars in her vision. Her efforts to twist free were met with more pressure from Terry's thick belly. He was momentarily focused on fondling her, and the relaxed pressure on her neck allowed her to draw several deep breaths.

"Like it?" Terry panted, as he looked deep into the anger that filled Sophie's eyes.

Sophie took a deep breath and spit into Terry's reddened face. "You bastard. Jeff will kill you for this!"

Terry took Sophie's nipple between his thumb and forefinger and squeezed down with all his raging might. As he moved back, he twisted and pulled as if trying to tear it from her body. Sophie screamed in pain and, as he pinched down harder, he threw back his head and gave a demonic laugh. He was almost at arm's length and Sophie grasped his hand with both of hers.

"How do you like it?" Terry growled, and Sophie thrust her knee into his groin.

His hold on her breast was broken, and he hit her hard across the face with the back of his hand. "I should just kill you and be done with it."

She turned and was half bent, leaning against the side of the car. Terry hit her hard in the ribs and she fell. "Next time, I'll give Melanie some of this." He grabbed his crotch and pumped up and down. "Or maybe Aaron would like some, too. He's more my taste anyway." He panted. "You didn't heed my warnings. Children or dogs, they're the same to me, remember that." Terry, still breathing hard, moved back and took in the scene. Sophie was lying on the ground, trying to get her breath. "I want the papers signed. This can only get worse for you." He turned and started back to his truck. "Skinning one of your brats would be a challenge, but I'm up to it."

SIXTEEN

The old green Volvo was gone. 313,000 miles, one engine, three sets of brakes, God knows how many sets of tires, two cassette players, and a year-old CD player. It was time for new brakes again, the engine burned oil, the tires were bald, and the CD player skipped every time he hit a pebble in the road. Just the same, Cole loved his old car.

The decision didn't come easy, but after his last trip to San Francisco, he knew she would never make it up and down all the hills, let alone the drive there. The final goodbye to Chicago was seeing the little black fart of oily smoke as the driver from "Kars 4 Kids" rounded the corner at the end of the block. Cole said goodbye to another friend.

With the help of several friends and a couple of fried chicken and spaghetti dinners from Olajean, all of Cole's earthly possessions were securely packed into his storage unit from PODS sitting at the curb. Within the next few minutes, the truck would arrive to load it up and send it on its way westward.

The final walk through the apartment was complete, and with it, a swelling of emotion. His suitcase with a week's worth of clothes and toiletries was in the trunk of his rented Toyota Corolla. He turned in his keys to Lilia Katz, the apartment manager. She gave Cole a brown paper bag of "little goodies" she had prepared for his trip.

"Long way to California, you might get hungry," she suggested as she handed him the grease-spotted bag. Lilia kept about six cats and always smelled of kitty litter. It was a nice gesture, but the bag and its contents would hit the first garbage can he came to, just the same.

His flight didn't leave until almost five o'clock. It was just a little past ten. Cole needed to do one more thing before he caught his plane, but it could wait for now. He took a seat on the stoop to wait for the truck.

The sun felt warm on his legs as he stretched them out in front of him. His thoughts replayed the events of the last couple of days. Some bitter, some sweet. The goodbyes were hard. The cards and tokens of friendship and outpouring of love let him know he would be missed. In all that happened, he really didn't think of those he was leaving behind and how his move might affect them.

He knew he would miss Olajean and Tom, that was a given, but he never realized how much Tom's wife meant to him. Of all the notes, cards and letters, hers touched him the deepest. Her letter spoke of her fondness for him and how much his friendship meant to Tom. She spoke of her concern for Cole and the prayers she offered up during his dark years. Most touching was her perspective on his reconnecting with Ellie and how her passing touched them. She wished him happiness and encouraged him to let Erin and her family fill the void in his heart. Most of all, and most surprising, was her encouragement that Cole finds a woman to share his life.

Cole took the sheet of flowered paper from his pocket and read the note again. "No one should be alone, Cole, and you have so much to offer a woman. I pray God gives you someone to walk through life with. From what you have told me of Ellie, I'm sure she would tell you the same thing. You'll always have a spot in your heart that only Ellie will fill, but a heart is a wonderful thing. There's always room for more love, and it never diminishes the love we already have. Stay well and you better call or write often!" Cole slipped the note back into his jacket pocket; of all the cards, it was the only one he kept.

The PODS truck arrived right on schedule. Cole verified his new address in San Francisco and the driver provided him with receipts and copies of delivery instructions. The driver made a point of letting Cole know that he was really lucky to get a pick-up on a Friday. If he was fishing for a tip, he was to be sorely disappointed. The entire process took less than five minutes, and soon Cole stood on the sidewalk beside his rental car, his last link to Chicago on the back of the truck. Cole took a deep breath; he was no longer a resident of Chicago.

Tonight, he would sleep in his apartment in San Francisco. Chris Ramos called to say that a bed was made up with new sheets and pillows, and the refrigerator was loaded with non-fat milk, Diet Coke, and cartons of Thai take-out. The cupboard, he promised, was well stocked with shredded wheat, corn flakes, and Rice Chex. Most importantly, there was a brand new 12-cup Cuisinart coffee maker, a pound of fine-ground hazelnut coffee, and a box of No Sugar Added Hot Cocoa mix. Cole would have all weekend to relax before beginning his first week at the *Chronicle*.

As he unlocked the Toyota's door the obnoxious overdriven notes of "California Here I Come" blared from his cell phone. A parting gift from one of his "happy helpers" no doubt. As usual, he fumbled, patted and panicked until he finally pulled it out of his pocket and flipped it open.

"Cole?" The voice was familiar, but he wasn't placing it.

"Yes," he replied, a little stronger than he intended.

"It's Sophie."

"Hi! I was getting in the car. All my stuff is on the road, and I'm officially moved out. What's up?"

"I just wanted to—" Sophie's voice trailed off.

"What's wrong?" Cole sensed the distress in her voice.

"It's Terry, he—"

"What is it, Sophie?"

"He came to the house. He attacked me. He's been arrested, but they let him go. I just don't understand. He threatened to kill the kids. He violated the restraining order, he hurt me, and they let him go!" The distress turned to anger.

"Are you all right? Where are the kids? Where's Jeff?" Cole spoke slowly and with all the concern he could convey.

"I'll be fine. The kids are fine. Jeff's outside. But they let him go! Cole, how can they do that? They said it was a technicality. What does that mean? He's out there; he could come back. He is so evil, Cole, he said he would skin my children." Sophie broke into sobs.

"I'll make a call and get back to you. Jeff's there and I know Terry won't do anything when he's there. He's a coward. I'm not going to say 'don't worry,' but believe me, Terry won't do anything when a man is around. Let's see what can be done. Go be with Jeff. Don't stay in the house alone with your worries. Promise?"

"Please, Cole, find out what went wrong. I am so afraid."

"I'll call you right back."

Cole called Tom Harris's cell phone to make sure he got hold of him right away. "Tom. Where are you?"

"In my office. You're supposed to be winging your way to the Golden Gate, aren't you?"

"I need you to check on something for me. Terry Kosciuszko," Cole spelled the last name, "got picked up for violation of a restraining order and assault. I'm guessing on the assault, but the restraining order for sure. Can you find out what happened?"

"Hold on."

It only took a couple of minutes for Harris to come back on the line. "I swear to God, Cole, sometimes I feel like I work with the Keystone friggin' Cops. It seems this guy nearly tears this woman's tit off and slugs her a couple of times. That's the assault part. There is a restraining order telling him to stay away from the whole family and their property. So, there's the violation.

"But get this, the Will County Sheriff's department goes to pick this guy up, and he tries to bolt back into the house. The deputies pursue and grab him. Once inside, they find all kinds of stuff—guns, kiddy porn, and all kinds of duplication equipment. They get so excited, they rough the guy up and forget to Mirandize him. Seems the guys they sent out were new on the job and well—" Harris paused. "Kosciuszko lawyered up. By the time the county guys sort it out, Kosciuszko has been released, gets home, and stashes any and everything incriminating. They come back with a warrant to a clean house. A real comedy of errors."

"So, where's it stand?" Cole asked, eyes closed, leaning against the car in disbelief of what he was hearing.

"He gets off. They are so red-faced they won't pursue any part of it for fear of incurring the DA's wrath after the first screw-up. What's your interest in this?"

"The woman is a friend of mine. She can't understand how he got away with attacking her."

"Makes two of us. His attorney must have really laid into them."

"This guy's nuts, he's not going to stop. Do we know anybody down there that could help?"

"Nobody."

"I'll let Sophie know the story. Not that it's going to make her feel any better. They are scared to death. She said he threatened to kill her kids."

"Great way to leave town, Sage. Sorry."

"You stay well, Tom."

"You too, buddy."

Cole planned to pay Terry Kosciuszko a visit before he left town. The dirty picture stunt was reason enough, but now he assaulted Sophie, threatened her children. Jeff was a good man and a good husband, but he either couldn't or wouldn't, do anything about his brother. If the system lets people like Sophie down, somebody had to step up and put a stop to it.

Cole warned him. Cole wasn't a violent man, but some people just needed to be taught a lesson. The strong must protect the weak; Cole saw it on the schoolyard of his elementary school, the mean streets of Chicago, and in the jungles of Southeast Asia: The bully became the agent of terror in the hearts and lives of those who couldn't fight back.

It was as though the people on the road knew Cole was on a mission. The traffic seemed to open up and push him along. The usual 45-minute drive to Plainfield only took 35. The radio in the rental car was clear and loud as the miles ticked by. Cole still didn't have a plan; he wasn't working on a plan. He was focused, mostly just staring ahead. He seemed to lose himself in the thunderous rolling beat of "Kashmir." The Led Zeppelin dirge segued into the ending medley from Abbey Road, and for nearly 20 minutes, there was no interruption. Finally, the pseudo-stoner voice of the announcer proclaimed it was another *Rock Block Weekend* and rattled through a promotional message about winning a Custom Harley Chopper if you were caller 69 when you heard "Born to Be Wild" played on the "Home of Classic Rock", but Cole didn't hear it.

The red Toyota Corolla idled just in front of the gate of the Kosciuszko farm. The large wooden gate was closed, and this time it was padlocked. On either side of the gate, the razor and hog wire fence stood as an ugly warning to passersby. A newly attached red-and-white NO TRESPASSING sign hung at an odd angle with a rusty piece of wire.

Cole pulled forward and nudged the gate with slow even pressure. He could hear the wood groan and the nails pull. A crack and a low screeching sound signaled that the rusty bolts were pulling out of the rotting 4-by-4 post on the right side of the gate. Cole kept his foot on the accelerator and slowly pushed forward. Not that it would have mattered anyway, but Cole completely forgot he was not in the old Volvo. A loud crack split the left gatepost, freed the old rusty hinges, and the gate fell flat in front of the car. Cole smiled, nodded at his victory over the padlock, and rolled over the gate.

Terry's old pickup sat parallel with the house and nearly against the front steps. Cole walked to the door and pounded on it with the side of his fist. He hardly hesitated before he pounded it again.

The clicking of locks was nearly drowned out by the cursing and grumbling from behind the door. "You better have a damn good explanation why you are trespassing on my property!"

Cole stepped back, and when the door showed the first sign of opening, he kicked it hard just below the doorknob. A dull thud reported the door hitting Terry in the head. Moments passed, and Cole stepped back, prepared to kick the door again, but it began to open. A fat red face was visible in the crack. Terry groaned, and the door flew open.

"Sage!" Terry bellowed from the doorway. A round red mark was beginning to swell up on Terry's forehead. His face was flush with anger.

"I got a visit from the police. Your little pack of perversity almost did the trick. Except for a lucky interception, I could have been in a most embarrassing situation." Cole inched closer as he spoke.

"I can't control the mail. 'Fraid I don't know what you're talking about anyway." Terry grinned, but his halting speech exposed his mind's futile attempt at finding an answer.

"I didn't say anything about the mail."

"I want you off my property. Now!" Terry was regaining his bravado.

"When I was here before, I told you to stay away from Sophie and Jeff."

Terry interrupted. "I just paid a friendly visit."

"She said you hurt her." Cole's anger was bubbling just beneath the surface.

Terry smirked and said sarcastically, "Just a little game of Tittie Twister. She's not really my type, too old, tits are too big. I wish Melanie would have been there. Then we could have played some really fun games."

Without thought or warning, Cole hit Terry hard in the nose. Terry threw his cupped hands over his broken nose and blood gushed from between his fingers.

Cole batted the fat man's hands away from his face. "Look at me!" Cole shouted. "This has gone from intercession to personal. This is *my* fight now. Sophie's out, Jeff's out, and the kids are not to—" Cole sputtered with anger. "The police screwed up. I am here to tell you I won't."

Cole slapped Terry's fat red face with a furious open hand. "You know what they call that on the streets of Chicago?" Cole slapped him again even harder and shouted. "Do you?"

Terry mumbled something unintelligible. He was crying.

Cole slapped him again with all the force of his rage. "We call it a bitch slap. I thought I would introduce you to it. See, you're going to go to jail. You're going to go for a long time, and your fat ass is going to be locked up with some very big, very black, very horny lifer who needs a cellmate to keep him company during those long, lonely prison nights. You'll be his bitch, and to keep you in line, he's going to slap you just like this." Cole slapped him again.

"I'll kill you," Terry blubbered through blood, snot, and tears.

"Please try!" Cole shouted as he backhanded Terry across the face.

Terry lunged at Cole, and Cole hit him hard across the jaw. The momentum of Terry's weight and the adrenalin-fed rage powering his attack provided enough power to knock Cole from the steps and against the back of the pick-up. The force knocked Cole's cell phone from his shirt pocket and into the dirt.

Terry punched Cole, landing blows to his ribs and shoulder. A glancing blow caught Cole in the side of the neck. Terry's arms flailed wildly, and Cole rolled out of the way of most of his punches. Terry fell against the bed of the pick-up. Cole was on him in an instant. He punched through the soft flab of Terry's back to hit his kidneys. He tried to roll the fat man, but he clung to the truck with all his might. Cole grabbed his wrist and, with a quick forceful wrenching, was able to twist Terry around. When he did, he saw urine running down the inside of his legs, and the front of Terry's green shorts was soaked.

"Sophie would have given you worse, but she couldn't. You're a coward. This is just the beginning. If I hear so much as a hint that you have made any contact with Sophie or her family, I'm coming back." Cole pulled his shirt away from his body and looked down at the bloody, snot-covered wet spot. "Thanks for the DNA sample. I'll be having it tested to get a match with the envelope you dropped off at the police station. You're through. No more *Red Hot Angels*."

Cole turned and bent to pick up his cell phone; in that instant, Terry grabbed the handle of a shovel in the back of the truck and struck Cole a thunderous blow to the back of his head.

SEVENTEEN

As his eyelids slowly parted, Cole saw nothing. The pain in his head brought an instant wave of nausea, and the slightest movement blasted white sparkling stars across his vision. Everything was black. Cole fell back into swirling darkness.

How long was he out? When Cole woke again, he was aware of a hard surface against his cheek. He rolled ever so slowly and put his hand on the back of his head. There was a lump the size of a hardboiled egg. Slowly, he opened his eyes and for a moment was gripped in panic. Was he blind? He blinked several times. Still, there was nothing but blackness.

He closed his eyes and felt his head a second time and gently ran his fingers over the lump. His hair was crusted with what he assumed was dried blood. The wound still oozed, and his fingers were wet with warm, sticky fluid. As he felt about, the surface around him was cold and damp. Cole turned his head slowly and saw a small slit of light above him. Then it was gone.

What he thought was blindness was total darkness. Feeling around him, he decided he was lying on a concrete floor. Cole carefully tried to stand. Slowly he brought himself up to his hands and knees. The pain in his head was excruciating, but he needed to stand up. First in a crouching position, then he stretched out his arms. He reached above his head; he felt nothing. With his hands still stretched above his head, he stood straight. He stretched his arms side to side and slowly turned. He didn't come in contact with anything, so he took a small step forward, again nothing. Slowly and carefully, he moved in the direction where he thought he had seen the light.

Then, there it was again. He shuffled at a snail's pace toward the sliver of light. His head pounded. The surface below his feet was rough, and twice he felt an uneven change in the floor. Cole froze when his foot hit something and it clattered in front of him. His breathing was quick and shallow. He kicked an empty beer or soda can. He continued forward. As he moved closer, the light widened. *If I am in a room,* he thought, *the light must be near the ceiling.*

With each step, he became more confident. With his right foot, he reached out and determined the path was clear, then in a shuffling step, moved ahead. He judged it to be about six to eight feet when his shins hit something hard. Cole bent and waved his hands in front of him until he hit something. It was wood. He felt the width of the surface, a little over three feet. He reached up and his hand struck another hard surface. He leaned forward, in front and above him was a third flat wooden surface. It was a staircase.

There was a handrail to his left and a wall on the right side of the steps. With handrail firmly in hand, Cole took the first step up. As he moved forward, it was clear that the light was coming from under a door. The stairs creaked and he moved slowly. In an effort to stop the creaking, Cole moved closer to the handrail and placed his hip firmly against it. As he moved up the stairs, he counted silently.

There were eleven steps to the door. The light was indeed coming from under the door. Cole leaned close and could see under the door into what he believed must be the kitchen. He could see yellowed beige linoleum and the bottoms of cupboards. To the left of the door, he could see the chrome legs of a table and chairs. The light seemed to be coming through a window. It was still daytime. Cole strained to hear something, anything, coming from the house, but there was nothing but the whirring of the refrigerator compressor.

He was in a basement or storm cellar. Kosciuszko knocked him out. He didn't see it coming, and he couldn't remember how he got down here. He had to get out. Cole took the doorknob firmly in hand and turned. Nothing, it didn't move at all. He pulled and the door gave about an eighth of an inch. The surface of the door was smooth and cool. This was no ordinary interior door. It was solid, and as Cole ran his hand under the crack, he could feel that it was at least two inches thick.

The frame on the door was a rough wood, unpainted and thick. Cole felt on either side of the door for a light switch but found nothing. There was no window or other light sources below him, confirming his suspicion that he was underground.

The bending and straining his eyes in the darkness made his headache worse. He turned and slowly lowered himself onto the top step. Elbows on knees, Cole rested his face against his palms. He closed his eyes and rocked gently with the throbbing of his head. He tried to think, tried to plan. He must come up with a way of getting out of the basement, but his head hurt so badly, his thoughts were scattered and he lost focus.

As he sat in the silence, fragments of images flashed in front of him. He remembered fighting with Terry Kosciuszko. For a while, he couldn't remember why. Then he remembered Sophie's call. What about his flight? He would surely have missed it by now, but it was still light outside. How long had he been in the cellar? He could not come up with how Terry could have hit him. Cole worried that his wound was serious. He was sure he was concussed, but his concern was the internal damage. His head ached deep inside, not just the lump on the back of his head. He knew that a blow to the head could easily cause swelling of the brain, and he also knew no medical care would be forthcoming.

The floor was cool, almost cold to the touch. *Perhaps,* he thought, *laying my head against the cold cement will help the swelling.* As he made his way back down the stairs, the sliver of light faded behind him. Within a few steps, he was cast back into complete darkness, but thankful with each step that the blackness was for want of light and not blindness as he first thought. When he reached the last step, Cole decided to explore his surroundings. With his right hand against the wall and his left moving from side to side in front of him, he began his way around the cellar.

Within a few feet of the stairs, he felt door hinges. Small hinges on what seemed to be plywood doors. His best guess was cabinets. He used both hands to trace the edge and soon came to a latch with a padlock. As he moved along the wall, he came to two more sets of doors. He was so focused on the last door that he ran into the opposing wall, striking his forehead.

Moving slowly and more carefully to his left, he discovered shelves. Twelve inches wide and about eight feet in length, the shelves were supported every three feet with metal brackets. Like a blind man at a market, Cole let his fingers explore the contents of the shelves. There were lots of boxes and cans. He smelled the cans and determined they were paint. The boxes were mostly filled with cups and glassware wrapped in newspaper. While unwrapping a feather-light, fist-sized wad of newspaper, he dropped its contents. The popping sound it made hitting the floor identified it as a Christmas tree ornament.

Cole's heart skipped a beat when he reached a large, flat, smooth surface; he identified it as a workbench. He searched frantically for tools. A hammer, wrench, screwdriver, anything he could use as a weapon. He searched the wall behind for anything hanging. Cole ran his hand over the wall behind the bench, feeling dozens of little holes. It was a pegboard, but there were no hooks or anything on it. He searched the shelves below; nothing but an oily rag. He pulled the leg of the workbench, thinking he found a club, but the four large lag bolts he found on each of the corners prevented its removal.

As he passed the workbench, Cole felt something loose and cloth-like at his feet. Kneeling, he felt the rough texture of burlap. He lifted part of the pile and counted as he dropped burlap bags to the workbench. A sharp pain in his hand was followed by a high-pitched squealing. As his hand made contact with a long boney sack of fur, a rat sunk its teeth into the fleshy part of his hand just below his wrist. He squeezed down hard on the rat's neck, but it wouldn't let go. Harder and harder he squeezed until he felt bones crack and its body go limp.

Cole cursed under his breath and threw the animal hard against the wall. Without thinking, he began sucking at the wound. Suddenly the fear of infection, rabies, or worse raced through Cole's mind, and he began to spit and wretch. He kicked at the stack of bags and heard a faint squeaking sound. The bags were a nest. Cole kicked and stomped the bags. He felt the soft squish of the squeaking baby rats under his feet.

The first batch of bags he picked up was safely on the workbench, but the bigger pile of sacks on the floor were no doubt covered in rat feces and the bloody remains of the nest he had stomped. The idea to use the large bags for warmth and to soften the hard cold floor now repulsed him. Perhaps later he would return to the five or six he had placed on the bench. For now, he moved on.

The wall opposite the staircase was bare except for a cabinet in the center. Again, Cole traced the doors until he found the latch; this time there was no padlock. The hinges squealed as he pulled one door open, then the other. The cabinet was about four feet wide and housed five shelves. Starting at the top, Cole examined each shelf. On the first shelf, there was a metallic tool or machine of some kind. He turned it in his hands and ran his fingers over the surface. There were perforations and ridges on the surface. A small knob on a short shaft that rotated was at one end. Cole couldn't figure out what it was. The second shelf was nearly full of jars.

As a boy, Cole often went to the basement of his aunt's house to get jars of canned peaches, apricots, and pears. It took only a moment for Cole to recognize the smooth flat lid and ridged screw-on rings atop one of the large glass jars. Without thinking, he unscrewed the ring and set it on the shelf. Just like when he was a kid and used to swipe jars of peaches from the basement and eat them with his cousin in the tree fort in the back yard, Cole slipped his fingernails under the lid and with slow even pressure, popped it up.

He raised the jar to his nose and sniffed. The smell was sweet and cool. He stuck the tip of his finger in the jar and tasted. The sugary syrup was smooth and refreshing on his tongue. Cole suddenly realized how thirsty he was. He put the jar to his lips and sipped.

Inside the jar were fat slices of peaches. The soft sweet flesh of the peaches felt cool and welcome in Cole's stomach. Again, he wondered how long he had been in the cellar. He put the lid and twist ring back on the jar and placed it on the right side of the shelf. He would finish it later. The rest of the shelves also contained canning jars. Cole nodded as he closed the cabinet doors, knowing there was food.

He was three-quarters of the way around the cellar walls. As he rounded the last corner, his foot hit something against the wall. Shoved tight into the corner were two boxes. The bottom box was heavy and sealed with what felt like duct tape. A smaller box sat on top, and as Cole felt the box and lifted gently, a lid slipped up and off the bottom section. Inside were five or six tubes, about an inch around and about a foot long. It was hard to tell what they weighed, but they were not hollow. Cole's first thought was that they were dynamite.

He tried to remember what he knew about explosives. He seemed to remember seeing dynamite packed in wooden boxes, not cardboard, and it was in layers of sawdust. Was his information from an old movie? Or did he read it? It just didn't seem to figure that someone even as demented as Terry would just store dynamite in a box in the cellar. Cole carefully ran his fingers over the tube in his hand. At one end there seemed to be a cap or lid. He gently turned the cap and it turned easily. It was a flare!

Cole quickly pulled the duct tape from the other box. Inside were chains, snow chains, no doubt he was right about the other box containing flares. He could have light. He removed the cap from the flare and felt for the striking surface. It only took two attempts until the cellar filled with the bright red phosphorus-fueled light from the flare. Cole could see the workbench, the cabinets, the stairs, and to the right of the stairs was the furnace and hot water heater.

He quickly returned to the cabinet with the canned peaches. Aside from the peaches, the shelves were stocked with berries, green beans, lima beans, and a tomato-based sauce of some kind. He wouldn't starve. He crossed to the burlap bags and quickly sorted the matted, chewed, bloody bags from the clean and stacked the clean bags on the workbench.

The heat from the flare was beginning to burn his hand. In the few moments left before he would have to drop the flare, he found an old rusty bucket beneath the water heater and dropped the flare into it. He could use the pail's handle to carry the flare's light around the cellar.

The center of the floor was mostly clear except for a pile of shelving boards and an old set of kitchen cabinet drawers and doors. Near the base of the stairs was a stain on the floor. It was his blood. On the wall opposite the workbench, an old table leaned against the wall. As the flare burned down, Cole searched frantically for something that could be used as a weapon, but it was no use. It was as though someone had cleared the room of anything that could be used or made into a weapon.

The flare sparked and sputtered as it began to burn out. Cole glanced around quickly making sure there was nothing he missed. As the flare flashed its dying light, he saw a bare light bulb above his head.

EIGHTEEN

Tom Harris was the picture of comfort. His wife went upstairs to the bedroom to watch *Desperate Housewives* and left him alone in peace to watch *Die Hard* on one of the "free this weekend" cable movie channels. He changed into an old pair of Kankakee Community College sweatpants he babied and protected since the days when he had played on the baseball team. Carefully balanced on the arm of his chair were a half bottle of Miller High Lite and a bag of thick-cut potato chips. Between his legs were a bowl of his special Cottage cheese, ranch and shrimp dip. He was totally in his element and savoring every moment of the last hours of the weekend. Then the phone rang.

"Yeah," Harris said, forewarning the caller he was not pleased with being disturbed.

"I'm trying to reach Tom Harris."

"I don't want any," Harris said, nearly hanging up.

"Wait! I'm not a salesman!" The voice pleaded.

"So?"

"This is Ben Mitchell in California, Cole Sage's son-in-law."

Harris grabbed the bowl of dip, took his legs off the ottoman, and sat up.

"Sorry, Ben. Usually, Sunday evening calls are telemarketers. Anything wrong?"

"Probably not, but I can't seem to reach Cole. We were going to surprise him at the airport and take him out to dinner. He wasn't on the flight he gave us, and he won't answer his cell phone. I hate to bother you, but yours is the only number I have in Chicago. Cole gave it to Erin in case of an emergency."

Harris cleared his throat. "I spoke with him on Friday morning, said he was killing time before his flight. Tell you what; I'll make some calls on this end, see what's up. He probably—" Harris paused. "He called me about an assault on a woman out in Will County. The guy walked, long story, maybe Cole stuck around to follow up. I'll do some checking."

"I'd appreciate it, my wife is really worried. Cole's usually pretty good about keeping in touch." Ben took a long breath. "You don't think—"

"Hey, Cole's a big boy. He probably put his phone in his carry-on and has forgotten all about it." Harris forced a laugh. He knew as well as Ben that one of Cole's biggest gripes in life was people who stood you up and didn't bother to call. "I'll call you in the morning. Where can I reach you?"

The son-in-law and the detective exchanged phone numbers and shallow reassurances that nothing was wrong. They both hung up dreading their next call.

***

Cole awoke to the sound of footsteps overhead. For a moment he lay perfectly still, not breathing, straining to hear what was happening above him. He recognized the clanging of pots and pans and the sliding in and out of the drawer below a stove. The footsteps back and forth above him must have been Kosciuszko's trips from the stove to the refrigerator and back. Cole rolled from his side to his back and winced at the pain and stiffness in his back and shoulders. He tried to stretch, and the movement awakened his full bladder.

Cole felt his way to the far corner of the cellar and peed in the pail with the extinguished flare. His body ached from standing and sitting on hard surfaces. He had fashioned a bed from burlap bags, but the cold damp concrete worked its way through the burlap, making sleep difficult.

In the darkness, time was a clock with no hands. Cole ran his hand across his chin and then his cheek. From the growth of the stubble, he estimated it to be least three days since he awoke in the cellar. By the activity above him, he knew it was morning. The footsteps were the first noise Kosciuszko had made since he had thrown Cole in the cellar.

After exploring the cellar, Cole sat in the darkness and tried to think of ways of using the items he had found as weapons, tools, or any purpose that would help him escape. The wood was too clumsy to use as a weapon. There were no sharp objects that would allow him to shape or cut the shelving boards. He thought of breaking a jar, but the size and shape of the canning jars would make them difficult, if not impossible, to break and use as weapons. To use them as a tool was equally impractical. The fear of cutting himself outweighed the limited use that broken glass would be on the inch thick lumber.

The flares provided the greatest potential, but his eyes would never adjust quickly enough for the element of surprise to make them effective in an attack. If and when Terry Kosciuszko ever opened the door, his eyes would be well adjusted to the light. Cole figured Terry would turn on the cellar light so the darkness would not work to his disadvantage. It was then Cole decided to remove the light bulb. The darkness was going to be his weapon.

Kosciuszko made no contact with Cole. The variables in his situation kept Cole's mind occupied and gave him focus and purpose as the hours rolled by. He played out dozens of scenarios, none of which worked to his benefit. He would simply have to wait until his captor communicated in some way. Terry, knowingly or not, prepared the perfect cell. There was nothing that could be used for any aggressive purpose and there was a supply of food that required no preparation or delivery to the prisoner.

Still, with all the variations he came up with and all the evaluations he did, the fact remained that the door could open at any moment, and Terry could just kill him.

What was the point of keeping him prisoner? Did Terry panic after hitting him? Maybe it was like a hit-and-run driver. Running away seems a good idea at the moment of panic but later becomes its own prison of fear and guilt. Terry hit him, knocked him out, and perhaps at first feared that he had killed him. Hide the body. The trouble is the body is alive. Ignore it and the problem doesn't exist.

If it was Monday, as Cole surmised, he was due at the *Chronicle*. Erin and Ben would have expected a call. Chris would have no doubt checked in to see how he liked his house. Chuck Waddell would expect him to pop into his office and report for his first day on the job. They would all have tried to call his cell.

Cole spent hours alone in the dark. Pain gave way to fear and fear to anger. His days and nights were completely jumbled. Sleep became an immeasurable blur. The lump on the back of his head was almost gone, and the blinding bursts of pain were now a dull ache. The terror of waking in total darkness eased as the hours passed, and he paced through the blackness measuring and touching and memorizing every inch of his basement confines. He was cold, and his joints and muscles ached from the hard damp surfaces on which he was forced to recline. He sat on the workbench with his knees pulled up under his chin. He tried to utilize the heat given off by the hot water heater, but its position in the room made close proximity difficult at best. He stood for a time with his back to the tank, but his legs soon grew too tired to stand any longer. The best position he found to rest was in a curled fetal position on the workbench, a roll of burlap bags under his head and covered by those remaining. This too was only a brief comfort because of his inability to stretch out.

The sound of footsteps above him, at first a thing of interest and alarm, now made him angry. Cole found the stairs and made his way up to the cellar door. He pounded the door with his fist and screamed.

"Kosciuszko! Let me out of here! You hear me! People are looking for me by now. You're only digging a deeper hole for yourself! Let me out!" Cole pounded again even harder.

Before he could move away, the heavy door flew open hard, hitting him and knocking him off balance. The force of the door sent him, arms flailing, backward off the small landing at the top of the stairs. He slid and stumbled down the first two steps, then lost his balance completely, falling backward. He grabbed for a spindle but couldn't get a tight enough grip to stop his fall. He rolled and kicked out hard with his right foot and caught a spindle. A sharp pain shot through the top of his foot, but it broke his fall. He grabbed a spindle with his left hand. Three steps from the floor, Cole rolled and scrambled to get to his feet. He could not let Terry reach him in a head-down position.

"Stay the hell away from the door!" The voice from the top of the stairs was like thunder bouncing off the walls of the cellar. "No one is going to find you here. Even if they look, there is no evidence of your being here. You're going to die alone and in the dark. If you touch the door again, I will add to the equation and make things a little more interesting for me and a hell of a lot more painful for you." With that, the door slammed shut, and the cellar was cast back into darkness.

***

To his neighbors, Terry Kosciuszko was the "nut down the road," "poor soul," or "the crazy bastard that destroyed that great little farm." When he strung razor wire at the top of the fence around his place, most saw it as evidence of how crazy he was. When he knocked down the barns and buildings, there were a few comments. By that time, neighbors were getting used to his strange behavior. So, when a couple sheriffs' cars were seen parked at the house, no one was surprised.

The sight of "Crazy Kosciuszko" tooling around the farm on his backhoe, digging holes or running trenches to nowhere was so commonplace that no one paid any attention to the huge hole he was digging in the back end of his property. There were lots of piles of dirt and lots of holes dug all over the place. Usually, he would use the big angle blade on the front of the tractor to bulldoze the dirt back in within a few days. No explanation sought or expected.

What none of the neighbors saw or would ever have imagined was that the swimming pool size crater was going to be the resting place for Cole's rental car. Late Sunday evening, Terry drove the red Corolla to the pit. He methodically removed the headlights, brake lights, and backup lights from the car. It only took two web pages and three blogs before he found instructions on how to disconnect the GPS in the car. By the dark of the moon, Terry Kosciuszko rolled the red Toyota Corolla into the pit.

The first thing the next morning, after shoving a few piles around on the front of the property, and filling in a long trench, Terry leveled the huge mound of dirt over the car. To prevent settling, he ran over the area several times, adding more and more soil. Satisfied that the ground above the car was packed and solid, Terry ran the plow over the whole back section of the farm. By lunchtime, the rental car completely disappeared and the back section of the farm looked ready to plant.

***

Monday morning, Tom Harris began making calls before he got to his office. Olajean Baker was nursing a bad cold and feeling too sick to make much out of Harris's call. She hadn't heard from Cole yet and didn't expect to for several days. She teased Harris a bit about "missing Cole already" but cut the call short when her phone lines started lighting up.

The airlines were a dead end. Cole did not check in, did not cancel or reschedule his flight. A check of the major airport car rental companies was more productive. Budget verified that Cole Sage rented a car from their downtown lot and would be returning the vehicle to the airport. As of nine o'clock, however, the Toyota Corolla had not been returned.

The two deputies Harris spoke with at the Will County Sheriff's Department were friendly and courteous but skittish about offering any information about Terry Kosciuszko. Harris was transferred to a lieutenant with no promise he would be more helpful.

"Martinelli."

"Good morning, this is Tom Harris, Chicago PD."

"What can I do for you?" The voice was friendly but all business.

"We have a missing person who has a connection to your boy Terry Kosciuszko."

"This one a pervert, too?" Martinelli's tone turned sour.

"How do you mean?"

"Kosciuszko's a pedophile. We could have got him on a major kiddy porn bust, but the two limp dicks I sent out there didn't read him his rights, so we come up with nothing."

"The missing person is a newspaperman, writes for the *Sentinel*. It seems he has a connection to the woman Kosciuszko attacked.

"What's the name?"

"Cole Sage." Harris felt a chill. There was a strange finality to giving Cole's name.

"Look, Harris, is it? We came up looking pretty stupid on our last outing with this guy and, frankly, my boss would have fired the bunch of us if it wouldn't have emptied the department. We are giving him a wide berth in hopes of nailing him on a variety of charges. What is it you think we can do for you? We're sure as hell not going to search his house if that's what you're thinkin'."

"No, no nothing like that." Harris realized he would get little if anything from Martinelli. "Maybe a drive-by? Sage was last known to be driving a red '09 Corolla, tag number ML938G. If you could have your people keep an eye out, it would be a great help. From what I hear, this guy's pretty nasty."

"Yeah, if you're a woman or a little kid. I'll have my guy in that area take a peek. Don't hold your breath. He's keeping a real low profile."

"Thanks, I'll check back in a day or two." Harris ended the call just as his other line rang. A Yellow Cab driver was found in an alley stabbed to death and underneath his cab. The search for Cole would have to wait awhile.

NINETEEN

Cole ran his fingers over the grooves he notched into the edge of the workbench. Seven notches in all since he began keeping track. The total was probably more like nine days in the cellar but he wasn't sure. His routine was pretty much set. The sound of Terry Kosciuszko stomping around in the kitchen signaled the beginning of a new day, or perhaps Cole imagined once or twice the end and it was the evening meal he heard. Once awake, Cole did 100 jumping jacks and as many sit-ups as he could stand.

His first meal of the day was the liquid from whatever jar he blindly chose from the cabinet. Sometimes he was pleased with the thick sweetness of fruit syrup and other times surprised and disappointed by either the salty tomato taste of chutney, a jar of stewed tomatoes, or the thin, watery taste of string bean juice.

The pail was reaching the three-quarter mark, and the smell was beginning to reach the farthest corners of the cellar. He kept his latrine covered with three of the dirty burlap bags, but the absence of fresh air left the stench to hover long after its use.

Occupying his mind was Cole's greatest challenge. His fear of death long ago dulled into an occasional wave of depression. He felt strong and agile from his exercise. His lack of calories reduced his girth by several inches already. But his mind began to play tricks on him. Several times a day, he found himself feeling his eyelids. He became so used to the dark, he couldn't tell if his eyes were open or closed. Except for the few hours of daylight that came from under the door—and then only if he was in the right spot in the room—Cole was in total and complete darkness. Then on what he figured was his tenth day in the darkness, he saw an old enemy walking towards him.

At first, Cole thought he was dreaming. The small Cambodian peasant, carrying a *Chinese* Type 56 SKS rifle, coming at him from across the room brought on such a panic that Cole swung wildly at him with a shelving board. The sight of Phoh, the guard at the Cambodian rebel camp where he had been held prisoner, reduced Cole to a shuddering, crying heap on the floor.

Near the end of his time in Southeast Asia, Cole went into the Cambodian jungle with a small unit of Pol Pot's Khmer Rouge regulars to see for himself the general's claim that the people in the backcountry were well served and protected by his men. It was anything but true. The second day of patrolling the hilly Tinh Bien district, the local resistance fighters had ambushed the patrol, killing everyone but Cole and the ranking officer. Lieutenant Him was later beheaded as a warning to Cole and the other prisoners in the camp that defiance would not be tolerated.

The guards were all hill people who watched as their families and, in some cases, entire villages were slaughtered by the Khmer Rouge. The appearance of a

CELLAR OF COLE

Westerner with the despised Khmer only reinforced their belief that the World was blind to their plight. In the three weeks he was held in the camp, Cole was beaten repeatedly and constantly subjected to interrogation. The man he saw coming through the darkness was the worst of the guards. He took great delight in urinating on Cole through the bamboo cage where he was held. This small man would wake the prisoner at all times of the night with jabs from the long thin bamboo sticks that he sharpened to long thin spikes as he sat crouched and watching hour after hour.

Cole was held for nearly a month before Colonel Khoeun and his men raided the camp and freed Cole and 29 other prisoners. The rebels who were not killed outright were forced to watch as Khoeun's men systematically and methodically murdered all the women and children in the camp and surrounding area. As soon as Cole was well enough to travel, he returned to Thailand and wrote the story on Pol Pot and the Khmer Rouge that won him his Pulitzer Prize. The return of the guard he called *Rat Eyes* was a nightmare Cole repressed for nearly twenty-five years. The shock of having hallucinations in the dark was a turning point in Cole's struggle to stay alive.

From that day on, Cole stayed focused and kept his mind busy. No more hours of staring into the dark. No more surrendering to the void. Cole was determined to exercise and condition his mind the way he conditioned his body. Along with his morning exercises, Cole began a time of prayer and meditation.

As he cooled down from his workout, he would pray for his family. For Erin to not be greatly pained by his disappearance; for Ben, that he would be kind and understanding with Erin, and for him to not give up hope. He prayed for his granddaughter Jenny, that she would grow up to be a strong, smart woman and that she would be a person that her grandmother would have been proud of. Cole prayed that God would help him find a way out of his captivity. He was not one given to prayer on a regular basis. In his prayer time, he often thought of Ellie. He believed that she was in heaven and wanted to pray that she was waiting for him, but was afraid that God would not honor such a selfish request. To keep from asking to be taken to heaven to be with Ellie, Cole would slip in the phrase from his childhood prayers, "If I should die before I wake I pray the Lord my soul to take." He felt childish and foolish for repeating those lines, especially since he had no intention of dying, but he wanted to have the peace that if anything happened to him, he would be reunited a second time with his beloved Ellie.

Cole often asked God to forgive him for only praying when he was in trouble or in pain. Cole struggled to remember all the words to the Lord's Prayer but would try interjecting phrases as they came to him. He always ended his time of prayer with "Thy will be done, on earth as it is in heaven". He couldn't tell how long he prayed each day, but he seemed to always *know* when he was done. He referred to these times as his "chats with God."

Hour after hour, Cole tried to occupy his mind with word games and memory tests. Each day, Cole would do three ABC lists. He would choose a topic, and then come up with one item for each letter of the alphabet. At first, they were relatively easy: shopping lists at the grocery store or mall, animals, famous people, and then they moved to more difficult subjects such as diseases, trees and plants, and nations of the world. His favorite was to list rock-and-roll bands in alphabetical order, movie stars, and movies. Sometimes, he would do it twice a day. Abba, Boston, Creedence Clearwater Revival, The Doors, Eagles, and always ending in either ZZ Top or Zappa. The trick was to come up with different bands for the rest of the alphabet. Aerosmith, Badfinger, Chicago. The trick was to not repeat his lists.

Cole actually enjoyed his other way to occupy his day. He referred to it as his "Memory Theatre." He would try to get as comfortable as possible leaning back against a wall or sitting on the workbench with his burlap pillow behind his back. The next hour or so would be spent replaying the memory of a special event or time in his life he cherished. He especially enjoyed reviewing his time with Ellie.

In the darkness, the images and memories played out just like movies on a screen. There were no distractions, no sounds, and no noises to disrupt Cole's thoughts. He saw clearly and vividly Ellie's room in the Eastwood Manor Convalescent Hospital. He saw her expression the first time he walked into her room. He relived their time together, making up for all the years apart, word by word, as best he could remember. Lying next to her on the bed and holding her in his arms as she slept, he could see her face and her eyes as he stared into the darkness, and he could hear her voice in his mind. Sometimes she said the sweet things she said to him long ago, and sometimes she spoke to him telling him not to give up hope. He could switch at will from their talks together as she was when he found her again to a time when they were young and she was healthy.

Some of the memories he watched were bittersweet. Since Cole was acting as the director of his "Memory Theater," he spliced together a memory of his life without Ellie with one of their long talks and he imagined he was telling her what happened.

On a warm day several years before they were reunited, Cole was eating his lunch in the park. Earlier in the day, he tried to find a phone number he shoved into his near bursting wallet, with no success. So, he propped open his Burger King bag and was sorting and tossing the outdated, unidentifiable and irrelevant contents of his wallet. As he sorted, tossed, and balanced the various scraps of paper receipts and notes, he came across the photo he kept of Ellie. The picture, faded and tattered, was of the beautiful girl standing on a rock with the Pacific Ocean behind her. It had been around the world and back. Through a dozen wallets, Cole carried the picture and, on those occasions where his sadness and longing for her overcame him, he would take the old photograph out and gaze on the features he knew so well.

It was spring, a time of rebirth and renewal. Cole was feeling bitter, angry, and alone. He looked at the girl in the pic-

ture and realized he was getting old. She was gone and would never return. He didn't even know where she was. Cole crumpled the lunch sack, stuck his wallet back in his pocket, and stood up.

Not far from where he stood, a crew of gardeners from the Parks Department was planting rose bushes. Cole walked to where they were working and, standing at the edge of a hole ready for a rose bush, he kissed the picture and dropped it in the hole just ahead of the burlap-wrapped roots the gardener firmly pressed into the hole. The man looked up quizzically at Cole.

"A funeral for old dreams. Where better than at the root of a rose?" Cole shrugged.

"Poetic. Now, you want to move back? You're standing on my dirt."

Cole chuckled at the memory in the dark and could have sworn he heard Ellie laugh, too.

The creaking of the floor above brought him back to the cellar and the reality of the dark prison that was his living nightmare.

TWENTY

It had been fifteen days since Ben first called Tom Harris. It was the third Sunday and the first time Ben didn't call for an update. There was no news and nothing to report on any of his calls. Cole Sage had simply disappeared. The Will County Sheriff's Department called back after a couple of days. Terry Kosciuszko evidently left town. Nobody had seen him for at least two weeks, and they were all the happier for it.

The car rental company was a bit red in the face to admit they didn't turn on the GPS in their rental cars until they were overdue. In the case of Cole's car, somebody must have forgotten to activate it, so there was no signal.

"Stuff like this happens all the time. Sometimes people disconnect them because they think it affects the mileage, or they think we're watching or will report them to their spouse. People are weird." The all-smiles-and-sunshine Airport Rental representative giggled. "We charge $200 if we catch them. But we usually don't."

Harris was at a loss. Cole's credit cards and bank accounts didn't show any activity. The *Sentinel* ran a front-page story with a photo of Cole about his disappearance. The phone lit up like Roman Candles for the first 24 hours, then nothing. The tip line recording filled up with "I will miss Sage, I loved his writing" running four-to-one over "I hate that guy, I hope he's dead." A few tips sounded promising but turned up descriptions only heavier or balder versions for Cole on their way to work, or living in the same house in the same neighborhood they lived in for twenty years. The tips faded away along with Tom Harris's hopes of finding his friend alive.

***

"Baby, baby, can't you hear my heartbeat," Cole sang quietly.

Herman's Hermits Greatest Hits was on the docket for today. Cole worked his way through his rock-and-roll ABC list artist by artist, singing as many of their songs as he could remember. Abba was impossible because he really couldn't remember any Abba song except "Dancing Queen", so he switched to the Allman Brothers. "Whipping Post" was infused with Cole's impersonation of Duane or Dickie Betts' extended guitar solos.

Cole became a student of the sounds of the house above him. Even in the darkness and, for the most part, complete silence, he could hear little subtle changes in the structure above. The vibration of the pipes when a toilet flushed or a shower ran. The creaking of the walls at night as the house cooled. The almost inaudible *poof* of the pilot light on the hot water heater detected even with the vibration of the shower water running. Footsteps, scooting of chairs, all made their special sounds.

The sounds were different for almost a week now, six days since Cole became aware of the changes. No toilet flushes, no showers, only what he believed to be daylight under the door. Terry Kosciuszko was not in the house. Two days earlier, Cole was so sure Terry was gone that he pounded on the door. There was no response. With each day of a quiet house, Cole grew more concerned that he had been abandoned. The jars of canned goods were beginning to run low. Cole gave up the pail toilet for all but bowel movements, and he began peeing in the empty Mason jars. The lids helped to contain some of the smell. He dreaded the day he would have to try emptying the pail into the jars. Then again, he hoped he would live that long.

Day fifteen, Cole fell asleep humming "Devil or Angel." He couldn't even attempt Uriah Heep and went straight to Bobby Vee. The sound in the distance, at first, played with the flow of his dream. He was walking along a dark street, following a small dog, when he turned the corner and was standing on the bank of a river. Even asleep, the change made no sense. Cole rolled over and bolted wide awake. The sound in his dream was the shower. Kosciuszko was back!

Cole lay still, listening to the low humming vibration of the pipes. What time was it? Cole stood and moved to where he should have been able to see light under the door. The cellar was black. It was nighttime.

The peace Cole felt for almost a week was shattered. The reality of his situation once again roared in his head. He made his way across the floor to the hot water heater. The surface of the fiberglass pad on the tank was smooth and slightly warm under Cole's hand.

The sound of water filling the tank was much louder than Cole ever heard it before. The thick insulation dampened the sound coming from behind the tank. Cole slid his hand around to the back of the tank and upward. The first pipe he felt was cold to the touch. The pipe below was hot and Cole could not leave his hand on it. Tapping in quick patting motions, he followed the pipe upward to where it went into the wall. Reversing the path, he followed the pipe to where it entered the top of the hot water heater. Cole moved his hand slowly and in a waving motion until he felt the cold, ridged surface of the gas line. He was suddenly struck with an idea.

The farm was far beyond the city limits and in Cole's mind, there was no way that gas lines would run this far out in the country. The line coming into the hot water heater had to be propane or butane.

Cole stood, hands at his sides, staring through the darkness at the hot water heater.

"What a stupid name. 'Hot water heater.' It doesn't heat hot water; it heats cold water." Cole's voice was calm and directed at the padded cylinder in front of him.

He ran his hand down the front of the tank until he felt a bulge under the pad. He pulled at the padding until he moved it above the bulging area. It was a faucet, with a small round handle; it was a release valve that was supposed to be used to flush the tank. No one ever did it, though, so the bottom of the tank filled with sludge and hard water deposits, making it harder and harder to heat the water and less energy efficient. *Out of sight, out of mind,* Cole thought.

He slowly twisted the handle of the faucet. It was stiff and probably had never been turned. As the handle gave way, the faucet spit blasts of hot liquid from the spigot. Cole quickly turned it off. He crouched and felt the floor under the faucet. Hot water mixed with a gritty, almost gummy solid. Cole laughed aloud.

Cole found it hard to sleep and several times got up and paced back and forth, sometimes mumbling to himself. A plan was forming, a thought really, just a seed of an idea, but as he turned it, twisted it, and spun it around in his mind, he came to the conclusion that it just might be his salvation.

The water heater combined two ingredients that simply didn't mix. Water quenches fire, but the butane flame contained by the tank burned hot. Water would protect him and the fire would save him.

Cole tried to keep to his daily regimen, but the excitement of his plan made it difficult. He completed his exercises, and his prayers were mostly beseeching the Almighty to allow his plan to work. His ABC list consisted of songs that motivated him. He jumped around a lot and finally realized he could only think of a dozen or so. As he paced and thought through his plan, he sang:

I see you got your fist out,
Say your peace and get out.
I guess I get the gist of it, but it's all right.
Sorry that you feel that way,
the only thing there is to say
is every silver lining's got a touch of grey.
I will get by. I will get by. I will get by.
I will survive.

Though he never considered himself a Deadhead, Cole was a big fan. He pictured the band on stage, tie-dye everywhere, and Jerry Garcia smiling out at him.

"Right, Jerry, I will survive!" Cole spun where he stood. "I will survive."

The pipes on the water heater cooled a bit, and the sounds above him died away. Cole was reaching behind the water heater, feeling the pipes and finding where they entered the wall when he heard footsteps above.

The door latches clicked and a wide swath of light crossed the floor of the cellar. Cole threw his hands over his eyes and squinted as he tried to peek through the slits between his fingers.

"Miss me?" the voice above him boomed. "Jeez, what the hell is that smell? You shit yourself?" Kosciuszko laughed. "Well, it won't be long now and all your needs for bodily function will be over."

There was a pause and Cole heard the low groan of the wooden steps as Terry came into the cellar. "Hey, where are you? You dead?"

Cole made his way along the wall and to the corner of the room and sat against the wall in the dark, away from the light. Suddenly a beam of light began flashing and jumping around the walls and floor. Moments later the light from a flashlight landed on Cole.

"You look like hell, newspaper hero." Terry laughed.

Cole extended his middle finger to the light and sang softly:

You can stand me up at the gates of Hell
But I won't back down.
Gonna stand my ground,
Won't be turned around,
And I'll keep this world from dragging me down.

"A last act of defiance? How fitting from the defender of the hopeless. Well, Mr. Wonderful, it won't be long now. Your ugly ass will be food for the worms." The light went out, the door slammed, and the sound of Kosciuszko's voice was silenced.

"You're right, fat boy, it won't be long now."

The boards that leaned against the wall were the only things keeping Cole from putting his plan into action. He needed to figure out a way to split a board lengthwise. He struck a board repeatedly on the corner of the workbench but succeeded only in breaking it in half. In desperation, Cole took one of the four remaining emergency flares and lit it and set it in an empty Mason jar. He slowly passed the board over the flame as close to the center of the board as possible.

As the flare burned down, inch-by-inch, foot-by-foot, Cole let the intense heat burn a path along the board. Back and forth, he slowly let the flame do the work of turning the shelf board into two long pieces divided by an inch-wide rut of charcoal. When the flare reached the halfway point, Cole flipped the board over and let the flame do its work on the reverse side of the wood. As the flare began to sputter to a finish, the end of the board was placed over the flare for the last bit of fire.

Cole stood once again in the darkness, the sweet smell of burning wood filling the cellar. He waved the shelf board through the air and watched the last orange specks of burning wood expand and die. He climbed up onto the workbench and carefully positioned the board along the edge. When Cole was certain the burned rut was exactly halfway extended over the edge, Cole stomped the overhanging portion of the board with all his might.

The sound of splitting wood was like a sweet song. Cole took a deep breath and stomped again. This time, he felt the wood give way. Cole hopped down from the bench and took the board in both hands, pushing the center against the workbench's sharp corner. The wood cracked and split more and more until it finally broke in two.

With his back against the far wall of the cellar, Cole ran his hand over the splintery edge of the split board. His plan to split the board worked exactly as expected. Now he would wait for the sound of the shower running.

To pass the time, Cole did his daily program of exercise, meditation, and memory games, but the time still seemed to crawl by. He sang as many songs about trains as he could remember. He imagined he was sitting in a boxcar door watching the Ohio Valley roll by. The farmland, rivers, and tall trees swaying in the breeze calmed his spirit. He hummed and sang "Hobo's Lullaby" until he drifted to sleep, hugging his split shelving board, the sweet smell of burned pine in his nostrils.

The sound of footsteps overhead woke Cole with a start. He heard the sound of water running, but it was the sink in the kitchen, not the shower.

"Go shower, you sweaty pig," Cole growled as he sat up and leaned against the wall. He picked up the split board and tried to think how to best use it if Kosciuszko were to come into the cellar. That wasn't going to be necessary, though. Because within a few minutes, the footsteps went away and the soft hum of the water running in the shower began. Cole went to the water heater and started stripping off the fiberglass insulation blanket. With an upward snap of the cover, he exposed the flame that heated the water. He waited and listened for the shower to be turned off. He walked back across the cellar and moved the box of flares to the workbench.

CELLAR OF COLE

The pipe gave a slight jerk and a shudder, and the sound of water leaving the water heater stopped, leaving only the sound of the water refilling the tank. Cole paced and counted, trying to determine how many minutes passed. His counting stopped when he heard footsteps again overhead. He was sure Terry was standing at the door. Cole's heart pounded in his chest. He passed the burned shelf board from one hand to the other. He tried to slip behind the stair rail, thinking he could trip Kosciuszko if he tried to enter the cellar. For a time, there was no sound at all, and then the footsteps moved away from the door and could no longer be heard.

Five minutes or more passed after the footsteps went away. Cole felt for the shut-off valve that controlled the gas flow into the water heater and turned it slowly. For an instant the flame got taller; he reversed the rotation of the valve and the blue flame danced until it disappeared. Then the pilot light flickered and died.

Cole turned the handle of the faucet until it was wide open. The hot water and sludge sputtered and spit, then turned to a steady stream of scalding water. Cole moved back so as not to get burned. After several minutes, he moved toward the water heater. The sound of water splashing against water signaled the sludge flushed out and there was a steady stream of clean water. His shoes splashed as he moved, and he could feel the heat of the water through his soles. He tentatively reached for the water; it was cold.

There was no sound above him. He moved the fiberglass side of the pad under the faucet to help dull the sound of the splashing water. Cole moved to the workbench and sat waiting for the water level to rise. He would reach down to the water with his burned shelf board from time to time to see if he could get any sense for how quickly the water was rising. In the cellar, there was nowhere for the water to drain, and the only question was how long it would take to reach a substantial level.

"How high's the water, Momma? Six feet high and risin'," Cole sang in a baritone impersonation of Johnny Cash. "How high's the water, Papa? Six feet high and risin'."

And the water did rise. Inch by inch, the sound of the water hitting water changed and Cole waited. The feel of the water changed, too. Cole's board began to move slower through the water as the depth and resistance grew.

Minute by minute and hour by hour, the water continued to rise until he heard the sound of water hitting water disappear. The water level reached the faucet. It was time.

Cole took the last three flares and two burlap bags and jumped down from the bench and into the water. The water in the cellar was just above his knees and Cole shuddered with the chill. He moved across the room to the water heater. As he waded across the cellar floor, a flare slipped from his hand and into the water. He grabbed and splashed at the water but the flare was gone, either sinking or floating away in the darkness.

The pipe, once so fiercely hot, was now cool enough for Cole to take in hand. Using it to pull himself up, Cole stood on the platform next to the water heater. He bent down and carefully removed the two flares. He felt the ceiling overhead and found the entry for the water pipes. With all his strength, he crouched and, putting his shoulder to the tank, shoved the water heater off the platform. The heavy metallic groan told Cole his plan was going to work. The pipes began to tear loose from the tank. Cole made his way to the stairs and laid the flare against the wall on a safe dry step. He turned and dipped the burlap bags into the water. He quickly moved to tuck the bags under the crack in the door.

Cole returned to the water heater and, hugging it with both arms, he twisted and pulled the tank until he felt it break free from the pipes. Water sprayed from the pipe that fed water to the tank. An elbow and a short section of pipe gave Cole a perfect way to twist the pipe enough to direct the flow of water away from him and the platform.

Using his length of shelving board, he wedged it width-wise under the ridged gas line just above where it entered the tank. Using the tank as a fulcrum, Cole forced down the board until he felt a section of the copper tubing give way. The section of tubing split at the seam and Cole pushed down harder. It would not tear free. He felt the gas line and found the tear. He took the line on either side of the split and began bending it back and forth. Faster and faster, he flexed the tube. He felt it grow warm, then hot in his hand. Faster and faster, he flexed the metal and slowly he could feel it bend farther and farther until finally, it broke in two.

He was at the halfway point. If Kosciuszko returned, Cole knew he was a dead man. Even so, he would not go without a fight. The end of the hot water return pipe had a small fitting still attached to it that Cole could not identify in the dark. Turning the cold water pipe was easy because of the elbow at the connection. Cole hoped and prayed the fitting would give him enough of a grasp to get the job done.

"Lefty loosey, Righty tighty," Cole said aloud as he gripped down on the fitting and began to turn.

He could not budge the pipe. He tried again and again. Finally, in desperation, he shoved his middle finger into the end of the pipe and gripped the fitting tightly with the palm of his hand. He took a deep breath and, as he slowly exhaled, gripped and twisted the pipe with all his strength. He felt it give. Ever so slightly, but it moved. Again he inhaled and let his breath out slowly, concentrating on turning the pipe. It was free. Now, grasping the pipe higher up, he unscrewed it from whatever fitting held it up in the wall above.

The last threads of the pipe unscrewed, and Cole felt it drop a bit. Gently he pulled the section of pipe from the ceiling. Cole felt for the hole left by the pipe. He felt air coming from the hole. He wasn't sure, but there seemed to be a space above the hole. Cole

CELLAR OF COLE

took the pipe and shoved it back up into the ceiling. He moved it from side to side. There was at least a foot on the right and five or six inches to the left. He dropped the pipe into the water, then got the flares from the steps.

With the cap removed from one of the flares, Cole gave the flare a twist. It did not light. Sparks flew and he twisted again and again, but the flare would not ignite. In a moment of anger, he threw the flare into the dark. Everything was riding on the fire the flare produced. Cole took the second and last flare in hand. He took a deep breath and twisted the cap. Instantly, a sharp pointed spear of light appeared. The flare fit into the hole in the ceiling with room to spare. Cole balanced the end of the flare on his index finger and with a sharp push shoved the flare up and through the hole and into the wall.

Cole moved quickly to find the flexible gas line and pushed it up inside the hole as far as it would reach. The pieces were in order and only lacking one element: the gas. The gas line was at least two feet above the flare. With a quick turn of the valve, Cole released the gas into the wall above. He opened the valve wide and then moved back to the far corner of the cellar.

Minutes passed with the sound of the hissing gas and sizzle of the flare, but the gas did not ignite. Then, when he thought his heart would burst in his chest with pounding, there was an explosion. Cole feared the deafening thunder of the explosion would bring the ceiling down, it didn't, but the roaring sound of fire filled the cellar.

Now if only the house fire would bring the fire department! Cole prayed the water in the cellar would give him protection from the heat. He rested his hope on the promise of heat rising. If the walls and roof caught fire first, if the neighbors saw the smoke and called the fire department, if the floor didn't catch fire first and fall in, he might live. It was the greatest gamble of his life, but he must try. To die trying to escape was a far better death than at the hands of Terry Kosciuszko.

TWENTY-ONE

As the fire above him raged, Cole sang at the top of his lungs "Amazing Grace," "God Bless America," and "My Sweet Lord" over and over with the occasional verse of The Talking Heads' "Burning Down the House," complete with a quivery David Byrne impression.

Cole resolved days ago that he was going to die. The fear that gripped him the first days of his captivity were long gone. If it were his time, he was ready. He already had several long conversations with the Almighty about his past transgressions and asked forgiveness. He mostly asked for the safety and happiness of his family and friends. In a selfish moment, he asked that when Ellie met him at the Pearly Gates she wears a yellow dress.

The heat that at first helped to counteract the chill of the cold water now reached the level where Cole needed to dip below the water to seek relief. The section of the ceiling where the flare and gas line was inserted burned through and Cole could see the orange flames devouring the walls above.

He sat with the water up to his neck and watched the orange flames bounce off the water and reflect onto the walls of the cellar. The ceiling directly above him, however, showed no sign of the fire yet.

As he sang, Cole wondered how far the flames had reached. Having never been in a house fire or, more specifically, having never set a house on fire, he had no idea how long it would take for someone to see smoke or flames.

As the water ran down his face, Cole realized that his quick dunks under were increasing from every few minutes to several times a minute. As he began to sing "This Land is Your Land," he thought he heard a different kind of sound above him. The roaring waves of the flames were joined by an almost harmony-like drone. Cole cupped his hands around his ears and focused with all his might on the hole above where the water heater stood. He was right, the sound *had* changed. As he stared into the orange inferno a large chunk of flaming debris fell through the hole and was extinguished in the water. The intensity of the flames in the hole changed too, and it seemed the cellar was growing darker.

Rising again from under the water, Cole ran his fingers through his hair. At first, he thought his eyes were playing tricks on him. Perhaps he stared into the flames too long. He wiped the water from his eyes and stood for the first time since the fire had started. There was water falling from the hole in the ceiling!

"I'm saved! I'm saved!" Cole began to jump up and down and splash in the water. He laughed, cried and then he laughed again. The flames in the ceiling went out. A shaft of light was coming through the hole above him. As Cole moved toward it, he heard footsteps overhead.

"Help! Can you hear me? In the cellar! Help!" Cole yelled up into the hole.

A moment later, a fireman appeared in the doorway at the top of the stairs. Cole raced up the stairs, taking them two at a time.

"What the hell were you doing down there?" A tall fireman in a dripping wet, yellow turn-out coat yelled through his air mask. "We gotta get you out of here. The whole back end of the house is about to fall down."

"Lead the way!" Cole called back, but he was already heading for the open kitchen door.

Cole got outside and found himself face to face with a group of firemen who looked at him like he had just risen from the dead.

"Where did you come from?" a tall man with a grey mustache asked.

"The basement," Cole said, his teeth suddenly starting to chatter.

"Get this guy a blanket!"

The grey mustached fireman introduced himself as Captain Jeff McNulty of the Volunteer Fire Company. He spoke as he watched his men still hosing down the back of the house. "What in the world were you doing in the basement?"

"What's the date?" Cole asked, still shivering.

"April twenty-first."

"I've been in there nineteen days. Kosciuszko..." Cole paused, "Kosciuszko knocked me in the head and I woke up down there." He smiled in amazement at how the fire was only burning the back end of the house.

Captain McNulty turned at the sound of sirens. "Now here are a couple of fellas that are going to want to talk to you."

The statement Cole made to the deputy sheriff was compelling enough to prompt the deputy to key his radio. "This is Constantine. I'm out at the Kosciuszko place. I have Cole Sage the missing newspaperman. Seems he's been out here locked up in the basement. Has anybody seen Terry Kosciuszko around town this morning?"

There was a long pause and then the radio crackled and a voice came through strong and clear, "That old piece of junk he drives is parked in the alley behind the office supply store."

"I think somebody needs to pick him up." The deputy smiled and nodded at Cole.

"With pleasure," the voice on the radio responded.

"And, if we still are sitting on that search warrant, you might want to get the judge to freshen up the date."

"I'll get right on it." This time a woman's voice responded.

"Mr. Sage, you look like you might like a bath and a change of clothes."

Cole ran a hand over his scruffy beard. "That would be really nice. But I would sure appreciate the use of a cell phone first. I have some folks that have probably given up hope on me that I would like to surprise."

The deputy took a cell phone from the clip on his belt and handed it to Cole. "Whaddya say we take a ride downtown?"

As the car pulled out onto the road, Cole looked back at the house. The firefighters still were spraying the blackened structure. The barren acreage looked even more desolate with the house in ruins.

"Can't say I'm sorry to see it burn. That sick son of a bitch has been a thorn in the side of this whole community out here for years. If you don't mind me askin', what were you doin' out here anyway?"

"He has been terrorizing some friends of mine. I was trying to..." Cole looked back at the house. A pillar of smoke was all that he could see. "I was trying to let him know that, law or no law, it was going to stop."

The deputy laughed. "You're the one that blacked his eyes and broke his nose?"

"I guess so."

"Must have been a hell of a punch. Yes, sir, it must have been a hell of a punch." The deputy stomped the gas pedal and hit the flashing lights.

Cole wasn't quite sure what to say when Tom Harris answered the phone, and for a moment he considered flipping the cell phone closed. Then Harris answered, "Hello, Lt. Harris."

"Tom, its Cole." A lump came up in Cole's throat. The impact of his freedom was just starting to hit him full-on.

"Cole? Where are you?" Harris sounded panicked.

"I'm in a Sheriff's Department cruiser heading into Plainfield."

"Are you alright? We thought…"

"I'm OK. A little pale, maybe." Cole took a deep breath, trying to calm his emotions. "How is Erin?"

"You haven't called her? She's been pretty upset, but she'll be a whole lot better now." Harris almost laughed with the excitement of the realization that Cole was alive.

"Any chance you could come and get me? I don't know where my car is."

"Where have you been?" Harris's question showed he was back to being a detective.

"I did something stupid. I came out here to confront Terry Kosciuszko and he clubbed me from behind. I woke up in the cellar of his house."

"How'd you get out?"

"I burned the house down." Cole glanced over at the deputy and he had a big smile across his face.

After finishing with Tom Harris, Cole rode in silence for a mile or two. The deputy sat next to him, humming a happy little refrain and tapping on the steering wheel. Cole was excited to let Erin know he was all right, but being free continued to sweep over him in emotional waves. One moment he felt like crying, the next like laughing out loud, and a moment later he felt like getting out and running next to the car.

His hand trembled a bit when he went to dial Erin's number. Twice he had to start again. Their relationship had grown so much since they were introduced as father and daughter. For Cole to have lived for over twenty years with no knowledge of Erin's existence only to meet her as a married woman with a small child still was a thrill of mixed emotions. Cole was sometimes bitter and angry that he missed her years of growing up and all the years he could have been with her mother but for his own foolish pride and stubbornness.

Then all that would wash away in the brilliance of her smile and the joy of having her in his life. Finally, he was part of a family, and he embraced the sense of belonging that she and her husband Ben gave him. Cole was thankful for every day they were allowed together. When his granddaughter Jenny was added to the mix it seemed almost too much for Cole to take in at times. Anyone who knew him would agree he lived in a sense of awe and delight that the little curly-headed girl called him Grandpa.

The phone at Erin's began to ring and Cole held his breath unknowingly. "Hello, Mitchell rezdense," Jenny answered brightly.

"Jenny, its Grandpa," Cole said softly.

The little girl didn't answer; she just began screaming "Mommy! Mommy! It's Grandpa!"

"Hello?" Erin sounded tentative and on the verge of tears.

"Hi sweetheart, it's Dad." Cole tried his best not to let his emotions show.

"Daddy, is it really you?" Erin began to cry.

Cole was unable to speak. For several long moments, they both wept silently. In the year since they were introduced, Erin never called Cole 'daddy'. It has always been 'Dad'.

A block from the Sheriff's Department, the deputy made a sharp turn down an alley.

"Where are we going?" Cole asked.

"Didn't you see all the news trucks? I thought you might want to clean up before you "meet the press".

"Yeah, I must look pretty scroungy," Cole said as he flipped down the sun visor and looked at his disheveled hair and beard.

"You look like you're about to run off and join Al Qaeda."

***

The drive to the airport was filled with war stories and the recollections by both Cole and Tom Harris of the first time they met. Beneath the laughter, though, there was a thread of sadness. Both knew they would always stay in touch, but the closeness and camaraderie they shared over the years were to be lost.

Marianne Harris gave Cole a warm embrace as boarding for his flight was called. The two old friends embraced with a bear hug and heavy pats on the back.

Then Cole walked to the gate in silence. As the dark-eyed departure attendant greeted him and took his boarding pass, Cole turned and gave Tom and Marianne a wave goodbye.

With no carry-on and no luggage, Cole felt strangely empty as he found his seat. As he watched the flight attendant assist his fellow passengers to their seats and help stow their backpacks and shopping bags in the overhead compartment, Cole wondered when they all got so old. He remembered always thinking how pretty the "stewardesses" were and how he shamelessly flirted with them. A smile slowly crossed his face as he realized that they all had grown old together.

"Paper, sir?"

"Sure." Cole smiled at the middle-aged woman who still worked the aisles with coffee, tea, or juice and a tired smile.

Cole was surprised to see the banner of the *Sentinel* as he unfolded the paper. He was even more surprised to see his picture jump off the front page at him. The deputy in Plainfield had taken him in the back door of the Sheriff's Department, but that wasn't enough to keep an industrious young photographer from getting a shot of Cole entering the building.

A picture of the burned-out house accompanied Cole's mangy portrait, along with a headline that read *Missing Journalist Burns Down House in Bold Escape*. The story, written by one of the paper's new hires, actually got most of the facts right:

Award-winning journalist and long-time Sentinel *contributor, Cole Sage, staged a daring escape from a house where he was being held hostage. In a statement from Will County Volunteer Fire Captain Jeffery McNulty, Mr. Sage set a fire utilizing the gas line of the hot water heater and an emergency roadside flare. Sage used the cold water line to flood the cellar giving him what he hoped would be a buffer of protection from the flames. He had been locked in the cellar since April 2nd.*

According to fire investigators, Sage took a dangerous gamble and had the fire gone the other direction, the structure would have collapsed into the cellar where Sage was being held hostage.

The owner of the house, Terry Kosciuszko, 36, has been arrested and charged with kidnapping, false imprisonment, and assault. In a strange twist of events, Mr. Kosciuszko has also been charged with a variety of violations of state, federal, and international laws including manufacturing, sales, and distribution of child pornography. Investigators from both the FBI and Interpol are pouring over what they are calling "a storehouse" of materials taken from the section of the house undamaged by the fire. Authorities would not comment on the report that Kosciuszko was linked to San Francisco child murderer Phillip Ashcroft.

As the plane lifted off Cole folded the paper and laid it in his lap and closed his eyes.

TWENTY-TWO

Every Thursday since his arrival in San Francisco, Cole met with Dr. Phyllis Katzenbaum. Seeking out counseling was not Cole's idea. Chuck Waddell insisted that Cole "at least talk to somebody" before he took on a full load at the paper. The first appointment was not productive in the eyes of patient or doctor. It was agreed that Cole needed another session. A little more time together would help them get closer and perhaps find a path to his recovery. Having a son-in-law that was a doctor closed the deal. Ben encouraged Cole to "lighten up and let the doctor do the heavy lifting".

In the second session, Cole admitted to having nightmares. His suppressed memories of his captivity in Cambodia that resurfaced in the cellar were addressed for the first time. He also confessed to finding it difficult to sleep unless the room was completely black. Dr. Katzenbaum convinced Cole it was a natural reaction to confinement.

She gave him several books and articles to read on people who were held under far worse conditions and the effect it had on them and their recovery. The readings gave Cole a sense of gratitude that his experience, though traumatic, was nothing in comparison to the people held in small confined areas in the dark for year after year. Add to their horror stories, torture, and sexual assault, and Cole's three weeks in the cellar were like a vacation.

Even though Chuck Waddell put Cole on short hours for the first couple of weeks, he spent a lot of time at home, drafting what would become a multi-part series on child abductions, murder, and the use of children in the sex trade. As a way of breaking from the oppressive nature of his research, Cole began to take long walks around the Marina District.

Living in a house was a new experience for Cole. He was an apartment dweller for so many years that not hearing doors slam and "things go bump" in the night took a bit of getting used to. Having the key to his own front door brought a sense of empowerment to Cole that he really enjoyed. He would never again have to wait for other people to collapse their umbrellas before he could get into the building. There was only one mailbox on the porch, instead of twenty on the wall in the lobby. Best of all, he could play his stereo or watch a movie with the surround sound on as loud as he wanted, day or night, breakfast, lunch, or dinner.

The San Francisco weather and the beauty of his neighborhood inspired Cole in another way too. He bought a bicycle. He felt silly and conspicuous at first, but soon realized he was only one of the dozens of people he saw every time he went out for a ride, and no one paid any attention to him.

The weight he lost in the cellar inspired him to try and keep it off, and the bike rides seemed to be helping. Maybe it was just the spring weather, the new job, the new city, or maybe a combination of the three, but Cole felt like he had a been given a new lease on life, and he was making the most of it.

Being close to Erin and her family was working another kind of magic in Cole's life. At first, he was afraid he would be a nuisance, so he tried not to call as often as he wanted. To his delight, Erin called him several times a week and invited him to lunch. A couple of times, she dropped over to bring him a casserole or pan of her enchiladas that he loved so much. Then there was Jenny. Her third birthday was in ten days. She had become Cole's world.

He loved to read her stories, take her to the park, and buy her ice cream cones. Being with Jenny in some small way was making up for having missed Erin's childhood. Twice Cole babysat Jenny when Ben and Erin went out. They watched *The Little Mermaid* and ate a whole bag of pretzels. Jenny sang the songs from the movie while dancing her Ariel doll across the back of the couch. When Cole tucked her into bed, they sang *Under the Sea,* and then with their own made-up lyrics to a hit-and-miss version of the melody. After she said her prayers and drifted to sleep, Cole sat on the edge of the bed for several minutes just looking at the miracle that was his granddaughter.

***

One quiet Thursday afternoon in early May, Cole was coming back from the break room after reheating his Mocha for the second time. A group of people was gathered around a TV monitor mounted on the wall. Cole joined the group even though he wasn't sure what the excitement was all about.

"What's going on?" Cole asked a woman at the back of the group.

"Phillip Ashcroft has killed himself."

Cole pressed closer to the monitor. The picture was of the cells in the county jail. Stock footage, but the voice-over was explaining how Phillip Ashcroft, the accused murderer of three little girls, used his bed sheet to fashion a noose and the top crossbar on the cell door to hang himself.

"No further details are available at this time. We now return you to our regular..." The voice on the television faded as Cole turned and walked back to his office.

The top of Cole's desk was covered in sheets of notes, drafts, and outlines neatly arranged in stacks in an effort to maintain some kind of coherent flow to the story he was writing. He looked at the phone and wanted to call someone to find out what the real story on Ashcroft was, but somehow he just didn't feel comfortable pursuing it. He looked at the monitor on his computer and tried to get back to work, but his head wasn't in it. The phone rang and the decision of what to do was no longer his.

"Cole, it's Ben. Have you heard the news? Ashcroft hanged himself; it just came over the radio."

"Yeah, I saw it on TV. Not much info, though. I was thinking of calling your buddy Leonard Chin," Cole replied.

"No need." The voice coming through the door startled Cole. Lieutenant Chin was standing at his desk.

"You're not going to believe this, he's standing right here."

"Well, that takes care of that. Let me know what he says, will you? I'm on my way home." Ben clicked off.

Cole stood and shook hands with the detective.

"I thought you might be interested in this." Chin handed Cole an envelope. "This was hung on the button of Ashcroft's shirt. It's addressed to you."

Cole indicated for Chin to sit down and then took a seat himself. He flipped open the envelope and slipped out the sheet of paper, unfolded it, and laid it flat on his desk. The handwriting was beautiful. Almost feminine in its flow, yet strong and square—much like the lettering Cole saw on architectural drawings.

The salutation was direct and surprisingly cordial in light of the fact that it was Cole who was so instrumental in Phillip Ashcroft's arrest.

My Dear Mr. Sage,

I write this letter to you with complete peace and resolve. You see me as a killer, a violator, or worse. The girls I released were saved from a life of spreading bitterness, hatred, and abuse. I saved the men in their lives from misery, yet I am seen as a monster.

You said that I need to let go of my anger. My anger was directed at a world of women that could not see that I was the same as the boy they loved at school. They saw only a balding man who would grow old alone. That was their loss.

You, no doubt, will write one of your famous in-depth articles on me and my so-called crimes. When you do, be sure to include the fact that my blood is on your hands. The ink on the paper they read is stained with my blood.

Yours is the pity, Mr. Sage, because you have killed a loving human being who only wanted the pure love of perfect little angels, and you brought that to an end. I curse you with my loneliness.

With sincere hatred of you and your deeds,
Phillip Wesley Ashcroft

Cole folded the letter and put it back in the envelope. "Did you read this?" Cole said, tapping the envelope against his finger.

"Yeah. I got it from one of our guys at the jail. We go way back. He knew we worked together bringing Ashcroft in. He wasn't sure what the media would do with it and thought you should have the first shot at it." Chin looked at Cole and raised his eyebrows.

"Tell him 'thanks'."

"I don't know if you've heard, but we found a direct link between Ashcroft and that guy that locked you in the cellar. Seems Ashcroft was a regular customer. There are emails between the two of them. They were hatching up a plan to video girls that Ashcroft was going to grab.

"If you hadn't put two and two together..." Chin cleared his throat. "There are a lot of people you saved from going through hell, Cole. I don't care what that piece of shit said in the letter, you're a hero in my book. The curse is on him."

Cole smiled at Chin and leaned forward. "I was thinking the other day. Ashcroft wanted to be remembered as some kind of "Angel of Salvation" for his victims. That whole thing of the three-name serial killer really meant a lot to him. The best thing we could do is not be a party to his fantasy. Like when *Rolling Stone* magazine pledged to never publish the name of the guy who killed John Lennon. He thought he would live forever. By robbing him of his name we sentence him to obscurity. I think we should just forget the name Phillip Wesley Ashcroft."

"Kind of a curse of loneliness all its own." Chin nodded.

Cole stood and walked over to the shredder, hit the button, and dropped the envelope into the revolving metallic teeth.

THE END

HELIX OF COLE

Exclusive sample from Book 3

ONE

Cole was sunk down in his overstuffed leather chair, feet up on the ottoman and a half-gallon carton of Breyer's Brownie Mud Pie ice cream in his lap. It was time for his annual viewing of *Woodstock*. With an eight-foot screen, 5.1 Surround Sound, and 500 watts of power putting him in the center of the Festival, he was missing only the rain, mud, and marijuana to make it just like the real thing. Cole was finally at home in his new house. He had found a kid at the *Chronicle* who was an electronics whiz and, with his help, Cole had his home theater system fine-tuned—looking and sounding 10 times better than it ever did in Chicago.

It had been more than a year since he moved to San Francisco. He never realized how much he hated the cold Chicago weather until he spent a winter in the City by the Bay. It had been a smart move. The *Sentinel* had gone through too many changes after Mick Brennan died. A couple of people had kept him up to date by e-mail, but as the months passed, the e-mails became few and far between. Now he seldom heard from the "Chicago Mob." The only one to stay in touch was Olajean. She e-mailed a couple of times a week and had even sent care packages of her oatmeal raisin cookies and a quart jar of barbecue sauce just in case, as she put it, "California barbecue isn't up to our standards."

Olajean was about the only person he really missed in Chicago. There was Tom Harris, too, but theirs was a different kind of relationship. During Cole's lowest times, Tom was always there with a "stop feeling sorry for yourself" or a swift kick to put Cole right. Cole had called Harris several times in the past year, twice just to get the legal angle on a story he was working on, the rest of the time just to say "hello." Tom's wife had sent Cole a gift certificate for movie rentals at Christmas and a nice card on his birthday.

Cole's house was in the Marina District and was costing a small fortune. Chris Ramos, the life-partner of Cole's new boss, had made good on his promise to find just the right place for him. The neighborhood was beautiful and pure San Francisco. From his front window, he could see San Francisco Bay and the Golden Gate Bridge. All the furniture Cole had moved from Chicago fit perfectly in the new place, and Chris was rather put out that his services as an interior decorator were not needed. Cole had taken Chris and Chuck to a Moroccan restaurant for dinner, and that seemed to smooth things over.

To his amazement, Cole bought a bicycle and had taken to riding around Crissy Field. He loved to see the sailboats on the bay and often stopped to watch people fly their kites. Last May, he got so enthused at the Festival of the Winds that he actually bought a kite and took part in the festivities. Every couple of weeks—weather permitting, which was almost always—Cole brought his granddaughter Jenny out to the spacious grassy field and flew the kite with her.

Most of all, he loved riding across the Golden Gate Bridge. Coming and going, Cole would stop in the middle of the bridge and watch the sailboats and windsurfers below. Once he was lucky enough to be on the bridge when a gigantic barge came under, headed for the Port of Oakland. Surrounded by tugboats and a Coast Guard escort, it was a magnificent sight. Coast Guard helicopters flew under the bridge, their blades painted with black and white stripes so that the whirling of the blades made an amazing circular pattern against the red-orange of the helicopter's body.

Cole had found a friendly market on Laguna not far from his house. He struck up a conversation one day with Carnell the butcher, and they had since become "baseball buddies." At least once a week, they'd go see the Giants play. Carnell always made sandwiches that they carried in. Filet mignon, Italian ham, and the best corned beef Cole ever tasted. Every game, Carnell brought the sandwiches, and Cole bought Carnell a couple of beers. Sometimes Cole picked up burritos from a Mexican place at 20th and Folsom, but most of the time he let Carnell do his magic. They sat in the cheap seats, and Carnell watched the game and Cole watched the people. They talked of politics, movies, and music. Both left rested and refreshed. Carnell Thomas was just the kind of friend who made Cole happy to be alive on a sunny day.

Work was going well, too. The fresh start had produced a new vibrancy to Cole's writing. The articles he had written in the last year were met with praise from the editorial staff and, as Chuck Waddell had promised, Cole was booked for appearances on several local morning television shows as well as interviews on CNN, MSNBC, and Fox News. The series he did on the dying fish industry brought attention to the plight of the disappearing generations-old industry in the San Francisco Bay. Cole had written about street gangs in Chinatown, the proposed needle exchange program in the Tenderloin, and the alarming increase in the suicide rate among Hispanic youth. But the article that had gotten the most attention was "The Path of the Pedophile." Granted, Cole's brush with death at the hands of his subject, Terry Kosciuszko, brought a bit more publicity than Cole would have preferred. The reaction in hate mail was far stronger than anyone had imagined. Because of the articles, the Cardoza-Worthington bill in the State Senate had brought new laws to protect children, mandating much heavier sentences in California for those producing child pornography. Overall, the reaction and renewed awareness of heinous sex crimes on children in the production of "kiddy porn" had made Cole's bumps and bruises seem trivial.

The new job had also brought several new friends into Cole's life and, for the first time in a long time, he actually had a social life. Thursday was poker night. The eight or so regulars rotated the game from home to home. Cole had even hosted a couple of times and pulled it off, to the compliments of all. Thanks to Carnell, he had prize-winning meat trays. Lucy at the Righteous Vegan Bakery recommended two different crunchy sandwich rolls, one with poppy seeds and the other with jalapeños and olives. She would've had a seizure had she known what was going into the rolls. A couple of jars of mayo, horseradish, mustard, and a head of lettuce, and "sandwiches at Cole's" were becoming legendary. Each week, five or six guys and three women bought in for 20 bucks and played poker like it was for a million dollars. It was BYOB, and the B was for beer, and there was no smoking allowed. They laughed, argued, and bluffed until 11 o'clock when win, lose, or draw, the game stopped and everybody went home.

At least one Sunday a month, Cole went with Carnell, his wife Lisa, and their twin boys Darnell and Arnell to one of the largest black churches in the city, True Hope Church of God in Christ. Cole got a healthy dose of gospel music and enough Hellfire and Damnation to at least keep him thinking about the straight and narrow until his next visit. After the service, there was always a big potluck lunch. The spread was amazing, and after at least two plates, Cole would slip out the side door and catch a cab home. Lisa would always scold Cole on his next visit and tell him he should have stayed for the evening services and got "the baptism." Cole would smile, nod, and look at his shoes while Carnell winked behind Lisa's back and gave Cole a thumbs up and a big grin.

The best thing about his move to California, though, was being close to Erin. They were now truly father and daughter. They seldom spoke of the past, living in the here and now, and were very happy. They frequently spoke on the phone, and Erin loved to pop in unexpectedly at Cole's house with a homemade casserole or a plate of enchiladas. They often met for lunch when Erin drove into the city, and Cole had joined her and Ben at several concerts, movies, and plays during the year. Cole used his press credentials shamelessly to get backstage so Erin could meet some of her favorite singers, and once he and Ben even bluffed their way into a speech by the president at the Commonwealth Club.

Cole was quite proud of his son-in-law the doctor and bragged about him frequently. Erin had stopped working and was dedicating herself to homeschooling Jenny. They had joined a co-operative of families who, like Erin and Ben, wanted to make sure their children received the best possible education but still wanted them to develop social skills.

The co-op provided social interaction through group outings to parks, museums, the aquarium, and the zoo. The parents came up with all kinds of field trips to businesses, farms, and factories. One of the favorite activities was to go where the parents worked. The parents were a diverse socioeconomic group, so the trips included everything from the sweet warm smell of sourdough at one family's bakery to the noisy clatter of a machine shop where one of the mothers worked. Jenny still talked about the day they rode on the cable car. The father of twins in the group was the conductor and let all the kids climb up on a box and clang the bell. In April, Ben gave a tour of the hospital with a goal of making it less frightening to the kids. They all went home in surgical masks and blue slip-on shoe covers. Jenny was thriving, and even though Cole was terribly prejudiced, he could see that his granddaughter was a very bright little girl. Cole had held her hand proudly as the co-op group toured the *Chronicle* one afternoon.

"I'm a farmer. I don't know how to speak to 20 people at one time, let alone a crowd like this." The crowd roared with approval and Cole thought he heard a ringing noise. He hit the TVs mute button, and a moment later the phone rang again. Cole jumped to his feet and picked up the phone from the kitchen counter just as the answering machine kicked on: "Hi, you've reached the other Cole Sage. Please leave his messages after the beep." He let the message finish, and then said, "Hello, hello?"

"Mr. Sage?"

"Speaking."

"This is Gerald Fonseca. I'm communications director with the National Center for Missing and Exploited Children. I'm sorry to disturb you on a Sunday afternoon."

"Not at all," Cole said with little conviction. He was getting a little weary that every organization on the planet was contacting him to speak at their meetings—for free, of course—or to endorse them or, worse yet, serve as honorary chairman of this or that.

"Well, maybe this will take the sting out of my interrupting your nap."

"*Woodstock*," Cole interrupted.

"Pardon?"

"Nothing, sorry, what were you saying?"

"On behalf of the NCMEC, it is my honor to inform you that you are the recipient of this year's Hope Award. The Hope Award is given to a person who has done an outstanding job of raising the awareness of the tragedy of missing and exploited children. We'd like to invite you to our annual awards ceremony so that the President can give you the award personally."

"Well, thank you"—long pause—"Mister—?"

"Fonseca."

"Yes, well, thank you. Who is your president?" Cole said, thinking of nothing else to say.

"That would be Franklin Evans, but I was referring to President Obama."

Cole stood staring at the paused image of John Sebastian in his silly tie-dyed shirt and pants on the wall-sized screen in front of him. "Wow, I, uh, I'm a bit taken aback. Thank you, Mr. Fonseca, I would be honored." Cole felt foolish and a little ashamed that he was abrupt at being disturbed. He stood gazing at the screen, hoping that irritation hadn't been too obvious.

"Excellent! The ceremony is the 23rd. I realize that's only three weeks away, and that's partially the reason I'm calling. It was the only date the President had open—actually, he had a cancellation but, anyway, we got him on board. We'll be sending you the formal invitation, tickets for your flight, and your hotel reservation information. Before the ceremony, there'll be a private meeting with the President along with the two other recipients of this year's award. We're grateful for your articles, Mr. Sage. We've seen nearly a 30% increase in hits to our web page and a substantial increase in donations. I look forward to seeing you in Washington. Good afternoon, Mr. Sage."

"Thank you, Mr. Fonseca. I'll see you there." Cole clicked off the phone. "Well, how 'bout that! Far around, far down, far up..." he said toward the screen in his best burned-out hippie impression. "What do you think about that, John?" The tied-dyed Sebastian stayed frozen on the screen as Cole smiled and said softly, "Well, how 'bout that."

Cole sat down and hit the play button on the DVD, but after about five minutes, he realized it was no use. The spell was broken, and he was far too excited to sit still for the rest of the movie. He had won awards before, lots in fact, but this was unexpected. It wasn't a journalism award, either. It was for benefiting someone else. And not to sound mercenary, but awards always meant that he got a raise. He was always happy to get them, and it was a nice honor, but they were just praise for doing his job. Now Cole reflected on what "doing his job" had meant. What had Fonseca said? A substantial increase in donations? That meant something. The other awards always came with a "making the public aware" tag, but this time it was measurable in dollars and cents. Cole was pleased. Self-consciously, he reached up and felt the back of his head. He slowly traced the scar that lay like a small, fat earthworm on his scalp.

The blow that sliced open his head had long healed, and Terry Kosciuszko was long dead, having hanged himself in his cell. But Camilla Salguero would never be whole again. She could never have a child, her body would never function normally and, worst of all, the scars in her heart, mind, and soul would never fully heal. Each time Cole touched his own scar, he thought of the little girl in the hospital bed. The last he heard, she was home. She couldn't go to school because she was terrified of going out of her house. Even though she had been told that the man who hurt her was dead, she was still afraid. In her child's mind, she was still unable to believe he was not outside waiting for her, waiting to hurt her again.

The ringing of the phone brought Cole from his thoughts. He hit pause on the remote.

"Yell-o," he said brightly.

"Cole?"

"Yes?"

"Hi, this is Kelly Mitchell, Ben's mom."

"Well, hello," Cole said cheerfully.

"Are you busy? Got a minute to talk?" The voice on the other end of the line was smooth and yet carried an air of confidence.

About the Author

Micheal Maxwell has traveled the globe on the lookout for strange sights, sounds, and people. His adventures have taken him from the Jungles of Ecuador and the Philippines to the top of the Eiffel Tower and the Golden Gate Bridge, and from the cave dwellings of Native Americans to The Kehlsteinhaus, Hitler's Eagles Nest! He's always looking for a story to tell and interesting people to meet.

Micheal Maxwell was taught the beauty and majesty of the English language by Bob Dylan, Robertson Davies, Charles Dickens, and Leonard Cohen.

Mr. Maxwell has dined with politicians, rock stars and beggars. He has rubbed shoulders with priests and murderers, surgeons and drug dealers, each one giving him a part of themselves that will live again in the pages of his books.

Micheal Maxwell has found a niche in the mystery, suspense, genre with The Cole Sage Series that gives readers an everyman hero, short on vices, long on compassion, and a sense of fair play, and the willingness to risk everything to right wrongs. The Cole Sage Series departs from the usual, heavily sexual, profanity-laced norm and gives readers character-driven stories, with twists, turns, and page-turning plot lines.

Micheal Maxwell writes from a life of love, music, film, and literature. Along with his lovely wife and travel partner, Janet, divide their time between a small town in the Sierra Nevada Mountains of California, and their lake home in Washington State.

Made in the USA
Columbia, SC
27 April 2021